Too Far from Home

A Breakthrough Book

No. 56

Too Far from Home

Stories by
T. N. R. Rogers

University of Missouri Press

Columbia, 1988

Library of Congress Cataloging-in-Publication Data

Rogers, T. N. R.
    Too far from home.
      (A Breakthrough book; no. 56)
      I. Title. II. Series.
PS3568.O4557T66   1988   813'.54   87-25514
ISBN 0-8262-0671-9 (alk. paper)

"Rainfall" appeared originally in *The North American Review;*
"Galb's Elbow" appeared originally in *Nimrod.* The author is
grateful as well to the Fine Arts Work Center in Provincetown
and the National Endowment for the Arts, from both of which
he received financial aid and encouragement.

The publication of this book has been supported by a grant
from the National Endowment for the Arts.

∞™ This paper meets the minimum requirements of
the American National Standard for Permanence of Paper
for Printed Library Materials, Z39.48, 1984.

To my parents,
and to Maureen and Joel

Contents

You Can Do Anything

The riders show up at the last moment, while Palmer is still sweating in the van after packing away Jackie's toys and the final few things he thinks Maggie may be needing. It's hot in there. The mailman has just come by with a letter from his mother, and as Palmer opens it Jackie runs out to him with an old board and a peanut-butter jar.

"Daddy, we almost forgot these!"

"We don't need all this junk, doodle."

"I like junk!"

Jackie has sometimes used this board as a roadway. Inside the peanut-butter jar Palmer sees a wooden bead, a piece of red plastic from a broken toy, two broken crayons, a bent plastic straw, three pennies, an old screweye, some pebbles, the yellowed filter of a cigarette—things Jackie has picked up on the sidewalk.

"Nothing more, doodle."

Palmer sits cross-legged on the carpeted platform in the back of the van with his letter while Jackie runs back into the house to look for more things to bring along.

Dear Robby,

It was good to hear your voice and to learn somewhat of your current plans. After ten years with Maggie at your side and four with little Jackie, I imagine there will be times of loneliness for you. It is true that life is unpredictable and one must adjust to whatever circumstances prevail. But our minds are empowered . . . .

Palmer shoves the letter into his pocket. A young man, scratching his black beard with his free hand, is peering in at him. He has a backpack on and under his arm he is carrying an open cardboard box at the top of which Palmer can see a pair of gleaming black cowboy boots, so small they must be a child's, studded with rhinestones.

"We saw your sign on the board."

"Gonna be leaving pretty soon," Palmer says, hopping down onto the grass. There is a woman on the sidewalk, too,

1

also with a backpack. Her eyes are focused somewhere a thousand miles away.

"I'm Craig. This is Berry. We're trying to get to Memphis."

"I'm leaving in about an hour," Palmer says.

Craig does not seem satisfied, and he sticks his fingers deeper into his beard. Berry is swathed in something vaguely oriental, like a sari, with overlappings of silken material, some of it the color of turquoise, some of it flowered with great red poppies, some of it a diaphanous black, and she holds a pair of ripe avocados against her flat belly, one in each hand, in a way that seems to imply they are as heavy as cannonballs. It takes her quite a while to focus her eyes on Palmer. Jackie comes running around the corner of the house with a couple of sticks and she looks at him instead.

"Memphis is right on your way," Craig tells Palmer sorrowfully.

"Jackie, we're not bringing sticks with us!"

"These aren't sticks! These are my guns!"

Berry, clinging to her avocados, comes down on her knee. "How old are you, sweetheart?"

"I'm not *talking* to you," Jackie says with sudden gravity. "I'm talking to my dad."

Berry sits in the grass and puts her avocados down and leans back against her pack. Her eyes go back to where they were before, to Memphis or the Gulf of Mexico.

"You can find more guns in Louisiana, doodle."

"These are *mine*."

Jackie holds them out and glares at Palmer ferociously. In a moment he scrambles into the van with them. He is naked except for a belt and a pair of shorts that are even more ragged and full of holes than the ones Palmer is wearing.

"We've got a son, too," Craig says. "Out in California. He's six."

As he talks about their son—talking about how they will be able to help take care of Jackie on the road because they have had plenty of experience with their own son—Craig keeps nodding his head and plucking at his beard and smiling ingratiatingly. Suddenly Palmer realizes Craig is trying to sell himself, like an applicant for a job, and he turns away with embarrassment.

"Just throw your things in the back," he says. "I'll take you to Memphis."

*   *   *

They are a hundred miles from home, passing dry cornfields from which big dark birds rise and wheel into the sky, and to Palmer's ear the throbbing of the engine has the rhythm of a song. It goes through his head again and again:

Goin down to Looziana, gonna get me: a mojo haaand.
Goin down Looziana . . . .

"*I* wanted to sit by the window," Jackie says.

"Well, doodle, Berry is sitting there now."

"Berry, I want to sit there."

"Tough."

She gathers herself around her avocados and stares out the window. There is a burned black barn next to the highway, its charred boards leaning into the weeds. There is a sign advertising Uncle Ed's Chewing Tobacco.

Jackie turns to her and bares his teeth menacingly.

"I'm strong. I'm the strongest person in the whole wide world."

"No you're not." She rolls her avocados into the glove compartment and arm-wrestles with him briefly. "See? You're not."

"I am too. Daddy! We forgot to bring my babies!"

"Doodle, I wouldn't forget your babies. They're right back there by the toolbox."

Jackie hops into the back, where Craig is sleeping, and brings his toy animals up front with him to the little red seat on the engine cover. His babies are a little brown elephant with a pink vest and a teddy bear with a green bow tie. He cradles them in his arms.

"*My* babies," he says.

They leave the cornfields and come into some woods. Berry begins to make sandwiches. Though Palmer isn't hungry, she hands him the first one—thick white bean sprouts floating in mayonnaise between two pieces of brown bread. Palmer holds it in one hand and drives with the other. Mayonnaise drips onto his thigh. When they come out of the woods, there is the river, blue and beautiful and wide.

"Daddy, is that the Mippysippy River?"

"That's it, doodle."

"When are we going to see Maggie?"

"It's a long river, doodle—we won't be seeing her today."

They are coming to a town. Beside the road Palmer sees a dead brown dog with big purple birds plucking at its entrails. He transfers the sandwich to his other hand and mayonnaise drips on his other thigh.

"Berry, I'm thirsty," Jackie says.

"Well?"

Palmer lets his arm dangle out the window. Mayonnaise splashes the side of the van; the bread bounces against a curb.

"I'm *thirsty*," Jackie repeats.

"I don't respond to *that* at all. You've got to say what you *want*."

"I'm thirsty of orange juice."

"You *want* some orange juice?"

"Yes."

"Listen," Palmer says, "would you mind getting him some orange juice?"

"I just think a kid should learn to ask for things in the right way," Berry says, reaching for the vacuum flask, "instead of all this bullshitting garbage."

*   *   *

Dear mama. So good of you to write. I'm not much of a correspondent, but I think of you. I haven't had a chance to read your letter yet as we've started the long trek south. I have a couple of riders. His mother died last week and they just came from her funeral. I guess they're okay, but . . .

Dear mama. I have packed Maggie's things into the back of the van and now I am heading south with Jackie. And I keep wondering . . .

Dear mama. Thanks for your letter. We . . . .

*   *   *

They arrive at the campground at nightfall. Craig brings out his cardboard box and stands at the picnic table looking into it. Berry is off in the bushes, looking for natural herbs. In a while Craig pulls out the little black rhinestoned boots and turns them over and over in his hands, gazing at them by the light of the gasoline lantern. Jackie, squatting on the hard ground near Palmer's feet with his dump truck, is collecting pebbles and sticks and cigarette butts and pieces of broken glass, and Palmer is looking up at the sky.

"When are we going to put the tent up, daddy?"

"Let's look for a good place for it, doodle."

It's a warm night, a beautiful night, with all the stars of the Milky Way floating over them like the afterimage of a great lacy wing. Jackie helps to put up the tent. Because it is September they have the campground all to themselves, and the only sounds are the sounds of cicadas, and treefrogs perhaps, and crickets, and somewhere the sounds of the highway, as muted and peaceful as the hiss of sea against sand.

"It's fun to go camping, isn't it, doodle?"

"When we get to Weziana we can all go camping, right, daddy? You and me and Maggie!"

"Maybe, doodle."

Berry comes back with a handful of maple leaves and Virginia creeper. She flings pieces of lettuce and avocado into a big wooden bowl and lubricates them with something the color of goose fat. She adds the maple leaves and the Virginia creeper and then mashes everything with a wooden pestle.

"Guacamole," she says. "It means Food of Life." She hands Jackie a little on the end of a spoon.

"*Yuk!*" He spits it out onto the ground and grimaces.

"Jackie, you didn't even taste it."

"I *did* taste it! It's *yukky!*"

Craig and Berry exchange a secretive look. Craig spreads guacamole on a piece of brown bread and stares off into space while he chews it.

"Delicious!" he says in a moment. "But maybe a *little* too much maple leaf."

"If it's good enough for the Indians it's good enough for me," Berry says.

She eats fast and angrily. Palmer makes Jackie a peanut-butter sandwich and brings out his mother's letter.

> . . . But our minds are empowered to direct circumstances to whatever we determine. "Do thou decree a thing and it shall be established unto you" (in the old Biblical language which is the language of poetry more than its modern translations). In any case it is sickness or health, happiness or misery—whatever you determine shall be your way of life. In medical terms nowadays health is dependent on stress and traumas in the field of psychiatry. So more and more the teachings or beliefs of Unity (mind over matter) are being accepted in fact.
>
> We were so happy to have had you all here a year ago . . . .

"Yurii is going to live in Minneapolis, right, dad?"

"Yes, doodle," Palmer says, putting the letter away again, "but you'll have new friends—you'll be going to a day-care in Louisiana."

"Who are my new friends going to be?"

"I don't know—but you always make new friends. Wherever you are."

Junebugs and moths are congregating around the lantern, and one strange little insect with red eyes is struggling in the guacamole like a brontosaurus at La Brea. Running her finger around the edge of the bowl, Berry begins to talk to Craig about why she is so tired. It's because of all the meat they ate, she says—that's got to be it.

"Can you believe my mother would have bought these things?" Craig says, holding out the rhinestone-studded cowboy boots. Berry stares at him with a look of surprising intensity.

"I believe it," she whispers. It's one thing to have been polite to his relatives, she says, but they should never have sold out like that—they should never have fucked up their systems with all those carcasses of dead animals that Craig's relatives liked to eat. All that saturated fat! All that dripping red meat!

"Man, as soon as we get back home," she tells him, "I'm going on nothing but fruit!"

Craig murmurs something Palmer cannot hear. A few minutes later they tell him it has been a long day and they are exhausted. They disappear into the back of the van to sleep. When they pull the door shut behind them, Palmer has a sudden perception that Craig and Berry are *good* and *decent* people; and this perception makes him feel very bad because for some reason he has just not been able to make himself like them. Why? he wonders. What is it that is lacking in him?

"Ur rurrr!" Jackie, on the ground behind him, drives his dump truck on its endless errands through the night, and Palmer sits at the table and watches the junebugs and the moths basking in the bright pulsating lantern light. And he tongues the words silently: *Good. Decent.*

"Almost time for us to get to bed too, Jackie."

There is nothing forceful in this statement, and if they were at home Jackie would go on playing without even hearing it. But now—is he really so tired?—he gets up without comment or complaint and goes to the tent with Palmer.

"Tomorrow we're going to see Maggie, right, daddy?"

"We've still got a long way to go, doodle."

They crawl into their sleeping bags, and Palmer finds that he is sleepy too, much more tired than he thought he was. Jackie suddenly thrashes around and sits up.

"My babies!"

"Just a second, doodle."

"I need my babies!"

Palmer crawls out in his underwear and finds his way through the darkness to the van. Should he knock at the door? But he is certain he can get to Jackie's babies without waking Berry and Craig. He opens the door. For a moment he stands there, trying to accustom his eyes to the pitch black inside the van, and then he reaches in, toward the corner by the toolbox. His hand encounters naked flesh. There is a sound like a sigh, and then he sees some shiny object—it is Craig's beard, moist and glistening . . . and now indeed he can make out Craig's entire face, with big soulful eyes looking up at Palmer like the eyes of a raccoon. And that flesh there, with its curly hairs, is the flesh of Berry's thigh.

"Jackie's babies," Palmer explains, in a whisper. He reaches over them and gets the little elephant and the bear with the green bow tie, then closes the door again. All he can think of is what hairy thighs that woman has; he's never seen such hairy thighs on a woman before—as if her pubic hair has spread like ivy and taken root all the way to her knees.

He brings the toy animals back to the tent, but Jackie is already asleep, curled on his side in the middle of the sleeping bag. Palmer puts them into the sleeping bag beside his son and tucks them in as carefully as he knows Jackie would want him to. Then he goes back to the picnic table and sits there for a while, in his underwear, in the dark, supporting his head with his hands.

It isn't the fact of his interruption of the private life of Berry and Craig that disturbs him, but the fact that it seems to him so ridiculous, so pedestrian, such a damn fool activity to be engaged in on a night like this, when the night is warm and the cicadas and crickets speak in the night air and the Milky Way is like a silver wing over all. Yet human beings are copulating everywhere, and animals, and moths and junebugs, crickets and cicadas, and even bears and elephants—everywhere, everywhere, under the great angel's wing.

Palmer crawls into the tent again. He lies on his back, and he stares into the blackness a long time, writing letters in his head, before he goes to sleep.

*   *   *

Berry thinks that eating eggs is just one more way of ripping off the animal kingdom, but Palmer has eggs and Jackie has an egg and Craig has an egg, and after they have cleaned the dishes and Palmer has put his gasoline stove away and packed the tent away and they have thrown away the leftover guacamole and everything else is packed away—after they have done everything and everybody else is all set to leave, Jackie is still kneeling at the side of the picnic table, driving his dump truck back and forth. Palmer stands over him, trying to

persuade him that it's time to go. First Jackie has to collect all
the little piles of junk, all the cigarette butts and bottle caps and
candy wrappers, that he has deposited in a symmetric
arrangement under the bench. Palmer sits down and lets him
take his time. Berry and Craig are already waiting in the van,
but it's a lovely morning out and it seems to Palmer there is no
need to hurry. Jackie needs some time to play alone.

At last Jackie drives his dump truck, with its cargo of pre-
cious junk, to the van, and they start off again. As they head
out toward the highway, Craig turns to Palmer with a look of
woe and astonishment.

"You've got a real King Tut on your hands!"

Palmer does not know what this means. He dismisses it with
a grin.

"*We* never used to spank *our* son either," Craig says in a few
minutes. He starts to talk about his son. One day the little boy
disappeared and he was gone all day and they called the police
and nobody knew where he was and late at night he wandered
in, a little boy of five, sucking on a lollipop, and when they
asked where he had been he told them he had just gone down
to the corner store.

"There was no *way* we could have just reasoned with him,"
Craig says.

"Well," Palmer says.

Craig yawns and looks out the window at the morning land-
scapes of Missouri. The highway takes them past St. Louis—
mist or smog catching the morning light like an emulsion of
silver in the air—and Jackie goes into the back for a while and
Berry, in the back, and Craig, in the front, are talking in low
tones about whatever they are talking about and Palmer is
thinking how many miles it is to Memphis and he is also thinking about Maggie for some reason, about the first time he saw
her, at the party in the prop-room downstairs from the university theater—everybody was a student in those days—and Palmer liked the way she moved, and something about her mouth
and something about her eyes, but he was embarrassed when
he tried to talk to her because all she could get out of her mouth
was stuttering, and he felt sorry for her, but later . . .

"What an energy rip-off this kid is!" Berry says suddenly.

What does she mean? It takes Palmer a moment to realize that her tone is one of exasperation. But what is she exasperated about? Has Jackie been asking her for a cookie? Has Jackie been telling her he's thirsty? Has Jackie been asking her for a glass of orange juice? A few minutes later, Berry leans forward and says:

"Rob, I hope I didn't offend you when I said that."

"Of*fend* me?" He keeps on smiling, and she is emboldened: "It's just that I think he's getting away with an awfully lot."

"*I'd* spank him!" Craig avers.

Palmer pulls over and stops for a hitchhiker. The hitchhiker is a young man with long blond hair under a huge floppy musketeer's hat with a big floppy pink feather from an egret or a flamingo's tail, and he is holding out a sign depicting a gigantic thumb. He climbs into the back. His name is Kim. He is coming from San Francisco—going to Memphis and then on to Florida—and then . . . . They are talking in the back of the van but Palmer cannot hear much of what they are saying over the sounds of the engine and the wind filling his ear. There is the smell of marijuana and then the strong smell of some sort of cheese—the hitchhiker is chopping off hunks of it with his hunting knife and making sandwiches.

Jackie sits on his little red seat again and the hitchhiker comes up front too. He talks to Palmer about the landscape, about the weather, about the people he has met. He has met such fine people, and the weather has been perfect, and this flat Missouri countryside (which stretches out for miles on either side of the highway like the worn linoleum on someone's kitchen floor, homely and warm) is fantastic—what a great place it would be for biking! Pedal your ten-speed all the way along the Mississippi . . . .

"Daddy! He said Mippysippy!" Jackie has to squint against the sun, and the sun glints in the dirty-blond ringlets of his hair. Palmer puts his hand on Jackie's shoulder for a moment fondly—rubs his thumb against the boy's nape.

"All the way, from top to bottom," Kim says. "You suppose you could do that? Go all the way from one end to another on a bike?"

"Sure," Palmer says. "Why not? You can do anything you want to do."

*   *   *

In the afternoon they are sleeping. Everybody is sleeping. The hitchhiker is sleeping in the front seat with his hat down over his eyes and Craig and Berry are sleeping in the back, but Jackie will not go to sleep. If Maggie were with them she would insist on it. And no buts about it.

"Get into the back," Palmer says lazily. "You need a nap."

"I don't either need a nap."

"Just lie down for a while. Just take a rest."

"I don't want to take a rest."

Palmer lets it go. But the sunlight and the thrum of the engine are narcotic; five minutes later Jackie's eyes are closing—he slumps forward and jerks back up again as he fights against sleep. Palmer has to shake him to wake him up.

"Come on," he says. "Right now. Get into the back. You need a nap. You're falling off the damn seat."

"It's not a damn seat either!"

"Jackie, if you don't get back there yourself I'll have to stop the car and carry you back there."

"If you carry me back I'm going to hop right up here again!"

"Jackie, look: everybody else is sleeping. There's plenty of room back there—you can just go back and lie down next to Craig. Just for a while. You don't even have to go to sleep."

"I don't want to lie next to Craig."

"Lie wherever you want."

"I don't like Craig."

"You need a rest!"

Palmer is strangling the steering wheel, and he is about to pull over to the side of the road. But Berry is awake. She leans forward and speaks soothingly.

"Come on, Jackie. Back here with us."

"I don't want to come back there with you."

"*I* think you need a nap."

All of a sudden she lifts him from his little red seat and hauls him into the back of the van.

"Daaaddy!" Jackie cries piteously.

"Thanks," Palmer says, but then he hears Berry give a loud gasp. He turns his head just long enough to see her slap Jackie's face.

"You little shit!" she says. "He bit me!"

She looks at her hand in astonishment, and Jackie scrambles up to his seat again. "Daddy, she *hit* me." Palmer says nothing. He keeps his eyes on the road. "I don't like Berry," Jackie says petulantly. Kim pushes his hat back from his forehead so he can see what is happening. In the back, Berry is showing Craig her wounded hand.

For a few more minutes, Palmer keeps on driving. Then he pulls over to the side of the road without warning.

"Okay," he says. "Get out." He doesn't look at anybody, and for a moment nobody understands whom he is talking to or what he is talking about.

"I don't *want* to get out," Jackie says.

"I'm not talking to you, I'm talking to her." Palmer turns in his seat and looks at Berry.

"What in heaven is going on?" Craig asks sleepily.

Berry gives an abrupt laugh and starts pulling her things together—her bag of dates, her low-fat mayonnaise—and shoving them into her backpack. Craig tries to reason with Palmer.

"This isn't right. It isn't fair. . . . You told us you'd take us to Memphis."

"Craig, for god's sake," Berry says.

Palmer ignores them both. The hitchhiker moves about a little uneasily in his seat, looking from one face to another.

"Daddy, I'm sorry!" Jackie says. "Don't make them go!"

"I'm not going to have people insulting my son, and I'm not going to have people hitting my son, and I'm not going to have people calling my son a shit!" Palmer says.

But Berry has already climbed out. She has her pack on her back and her fists in her pants pockets, and she is looking away from him at the flow of oncoming traffic. Craig follows her reluctantly. He grabs his pack and his cardboard box.

"Well, I guess that's it," he says.

"If your wife would like to apologize to Jackie I'll give you a ride to Memphis."

Craig closes the van door gently, as though he is still trying to sell himself. A stone hits the roof of the van as Palmer drives away.

"Why couldn't they come with us, daddy?"

"I won't have people insulting you, doodle."

At the first exit, Palmer turns the van around and heads north again. The hitchhiker says nothing. Palmer does not see them.

"We were just here!" Jackie says.

Palmer drives past one turnoff . . . past another. Finally he turns south again. Right there—a little before that big sign, and with that white farmhouse off in the distance, past a yellowing field of soybeans—that is where he let them off, but they are not there now.

"Well, I don't see them, doodle."

"Where are they?"

"I guess they decided to get a ride with somebody else."

"Why?"

"They'll probably get to Memphis faster with somebody else. Jackie, I wish to Christ you would stop biting people! We've been telling you that ever since you got teeth—I don't know why you keep doing it!"

"She hit me."

"Doodle, she hit you because you bit her! *Any*body's going to hit you if you bite them."

*   *   *

For two hours Palmer waits for somebody to call him a son of a bitch. He feels as though the words have already been uttered and they are hovering in the air beside him like gnats, just waiting to dart into his ear and make themselves known. The words buzz and buzz around his head, but Jackie, on the seat beside him, is saying only gentle words to his babies, the bear with the green bow tie and the elephant with the pink vest, and Kim has his feet up on the dashboard and his musketeer's hat down over his eyes and he is saying nothing. Perhaps he is asleep. Palmer believes he is meditating secretly on injustice and cruelty. But when they cross the bridge to Memphis, Kim lifts the brim of his hat and peers out at the Mississippi.

"Listen," he says, "I was thinking maybe I'll ride on down to Louisiana with you. Will that be all right?"

"Sure."

There is a lump in Palmer's throat, and for a moment he can say nothing more. It is as if this man has just declared love and undying loyalty to him. He follows the highway signs. The curves and loops of the highway take him past Memphis and head him down toward Mississippi.

"Listen," Palmer says. "Sometimes I do things I shouldn't do. You know? I'm not a vegetarian. I eat meat, and maybe . . . maybe you get angry more when you eat meat. Maybe there's too much high-quality protein in my diet."

"I'm not judging you, man. I don't judge." Kim takes off his hat, shakes his head, moves his hat around in his hands and looks at it from all angles. Finally he puts it on again and looks out the window. "I just let things happen. I just watch and learn."

*   *   *

They stop for the night by a reservoir in northern Mississippi. Jackie adores Kim. He follows him around like a puppy. When Kim says, "Stop following me around or I'll kick your butt," it only increases Jackie's devotion. Kim is building a fire, and Jackie picks up pieces of wood and brings them to him.

"Kim, is this piece okay?"

"Sure, that's just fine."

"How about this piece, Kim?"

"Great."

Lying in the sleeping bag later, with his elephant and his bear cradled in his arms, Jackie murmurs, "Is Kim going to Weziana with us?" but he is asleep before Palmer can give him an answer. In the morning Palmer says, "You like Kim, don't

you, doodle? He seems easier to get along with than Berry and
Craig."

"I like Craig and Berry and cousin Stephie and cousin Jan."

"That's good, Jackie—you like everybody."

"I don't like *every*body."

And the green trees lining the highway are silvered with the
dew of morning and there is the smell of pines and dew and
the smell of morning in the air as they drive on, and Kim is
turning into Jackie's big brother. He is letting Jackie wear his
floppy hat and he is drawing pictures for Jackie in a sketch-
book he had in his pack, cartoon pictures of grizzly bears and
tramps and firemen and elephants with huge white tusks and
even a cartoon of Jackie himself, with his head covered with a
radiant mop of curls and stars for eyes.

Palmer slows unwillingly for another hitchhiker. He has a
suitcase about large enough for a pair of pajamas, and he looks
dark and sinister. Maybe he is the terrible stranger. Maybe that
little suitcase of his is filled with terrible sharp knives; maybe
he is the man you have read about, in the newspapers and in
Krafft-Ebing, who will chop you into tiny morsels and mail
them to members of congress, or else, while his hogs are root-
ing about in the moist cavern behind your ribs, will write
down in his diary how it felt to tie your naked arteries into
knots with his bare fingers.

But that is no reason for not picking a man up. How could
you explain it to Kim? If you pick up one hitchhiker, you've got
to stop for all of them—they're all brothers under the skin.
Anyway, it is too late. The hitchhiker already is opening the
door and climbing into the back.

"Mighty nice of you to stop?"

He has a broad smile and a broad southern accent that
makes every sentence sound like a question.

"Ah'm Sonny? and ah'm heading towahds New Awleans?"

Kim turns around in his seat and pretty soon the two of
them are swapping hitchhiker stories, which have to do with
"Wheah *you* from?" and "Took me two days to get from California to St. Louis."

"You all leave theah this morning?"

"Naw."

"Ah was up theah in Memphis? Mah money run out, so ah have to ride mah thumb?"

A road sign flashes past, and Sonny starts to talk about Jackson, Mississippi.

"You doan want to stop theah, son," he tells Kim.

"I wasn't going to."

"Ah love that town like mah sister, but they doan like hippies theah? Full of rednecks? They think anyone with his hair down to his ears is a hippie." Sonny laughs long and slow. "You wouldn't last two seconds theah," he says, snapping his fingers.

"But I've heard good things about New Orleans."

"That ain't such a bad place to be."

Sonny opens his suitcase and there is nothing in it except a radio and a big plastic bag of marijuana. The radio doesn't work inside the van—it just makes a crackling noise. Sonny throws it back into his suitcase and he and Kim talk to each other about marijuana, and then they smoke some marijuana and they talk about the cost of marijuana and about the quality of marijuana and about the amusing things that can happen to a hitchhiker who is carrying marijuana.

"Well, I've got some cheese here," Kim says, rummaging around in his backpack.

"Ah believe ah could use some of that." Sonny is quiet for a moment and then he gives a deep sigh. "Now that doan taste half bad, but it sure doan smell like roses."

"It's made without rennet."

"So is this marijuana," Sonny says. "Not a drop of rennet in it."

"Rennet is something they put in cheese," Kim says. "But they have to kill a cow to get the rennet."

Sonny laughs with the same sort of dry, crackling noise his radio made.

"Boy, you have made some cow very happy."

"And I've got some pine nuts here too—"

"Hell," Sonny says, taking a handful of pine nuts, "you would not even last *one* second in Jackson."

"Mankind's only perfect food," Kim says happily.

"Daddy, I want some orange juice," Jackie says.

"Okay, doodle."

"I think homegrown dope is the best," Kim says. "It always gives me the best high—it's got so much *love* in it."

"Plenty of magic mushrooms around here—"

"I always wanted to try those."

Sonny talks about the magic mushrooms, which pop up out of the Mississippi soil after the rain—you can tell them by the light blue ring around their top. The ones without the blue ring are deadly poisonous.

"You ever take peyote?"

But Sonny does not answer. He is looking out the window. They are passing a crossroads, down below the highway—a couple of houses, a gas station, a few people and dogs.

"Wee-ooo!" Sonny says, turning toward Palmer. "Did you see that?"

"Nice, huh?"

"I doan like black people, but I *doan* mind some of their ladies."

"Daddy, I got to go bowm."

"Why didn't you go when we stopped for gas, doodle? . . . Never mind."

"Why don't you like black people?" Kim asks.

Palmer pulls off the highway at a rest area. It is good to get out of the car. On the way to the little wooden house, Jackie stops and looks at an old black man who has been watering the lawn—a man who is lean and strong, though a little bent, and whose face is sullen and whose entire body seems suffused with a silent anger. His right arm is missing below the elbow. Jackie stares at him and stares at him.

"Let's go, doodle."

Jackie comes along reluctantly and they go on down the path. The day is getting hot and there is a smell of flowers and another smell that is like the smell of hot tar.

"You were looking at that man because part of his arm is missing, huh, doodle?"

Jackie is shy about it, and Palmer tells him that these things happen sometimes, that people have accidents, that his grandfather, for instance, lost parts of three fingers in an airplane propeller and that Pieta's father chopped off part of his thumb when he was working in a meat-packing plant.

"That's why I tell you not to play with sticks sometimes, doodle. Sometimes people lose their eyes."

The roof of the little wooden house is made of greenish corrugated plastic. Sunlight comes through the roof and makes everything look green inside. Jackie peers down the hole.

"That's where the poop goes, right, dad?"

"Yes, Jackie—you know that."

"Remember when Yurii threw my shirt down the hole?"

"There wasn't anything funny about it, doodle."

Palmer leans against the whitewashed wood and waits for his son to finish. There are graffiti everywhere. Above the tin urinal someone has written "Jesus eats shit" and someone else has written "Ecology or death" and someone else has written "A man is just a fool and a woman's tool." There is a little window, above these graffiti, covered with two layers of screening. Between the layers is an aggregation of dead flies and moths and hornets and junebugs, and on the outside a couple of other flies are clinging to the screen and looking in.

"Daddy, can we go camping in Weziana?"

"Sometime, doodle."

"Can we go to California after we go to Weziana?"

"It'd be nice to go there sometime."

Kim and Sonny are sitting at one of the concrete picnic tables beneath a great green overhanging tree, and smatterings of sunlight fall upon them through the leaves, flashes of sunlight like little gold fishes, swimming back and forth, back and forth, with every change in the breeze. Sonny's radio is making music now and he is using it as a pillow. Kim, hacking off tiny pieces from the remaining cube of cheese, nags him gently:

"Well, how about their music? Don't you like their music?"

"Ah can get along with theah music. But that doan mean ah have to like *them*."

Kim skewers the last piece of cheese on the point of his knife and holds it out to Palmer. Palmer isn't hungry. Kim plunges it into his own mouth, and when it is all gone Jackie says sorrowfully, "*I* didn't get any."

"There isn't any more, doodle—I'll make you a peanut-butter sandwich."

"I don't *want* a peanut-butter sandwich."

He likes them as individuals, Sonny says, getting to his feet, but not as a people. They just aren't people you can rely on.

"But they have some mighty nice parties," he says.

They go back to the van and Palmer heads it out onto the highway again.

"You got to get into a few fights?" Sonny continues, grinning happily. "But once they find out you can take care of yourself, everything they have is youahs. Their wine, their women—everything."

"Well then," Kim says, "I don't understand—"

"As individuals," Sonny says softly, "theyah okay."

His smile fills the van. And Kim brings out a kazoo and starts to play some music such as you might hear in a nightclub in New Orleans if everything was joyful and the people in New Orleans played kazoos.

*   *   *

Dear mama. Let me just tell you this straight out. Maggie and I are not the ideal couple. We don't want each other any more, we don't care about each other, we—

O mama, I can't tell you about it, I can't tell you anything at all! But how long am I supposed to keep pretending that everything is fine?

*   *   *

The road divides. One way goes to New Orleans and the other way goes to Maggie. Palmer stops to let the hitchhikers out. Jackie climbs out the window and onto the roof of the van and sits there, laughing and shouting, while Palmer is bidding them adieu.

"Daddy! Look at me!"

"I see you, doodle."

Palmer feels almost like weeping. It is as if these two fine gentlemen were lifelong friends of his, and he is telling them good-bye forever. But for Jackie their departure is nothing. It means only that the seat by the window is free, for the first time in a thousand miles—Jackie sits there with his elephant and his bear, looking out sleepily at the lush foliage of Louisiana.

"I want to stop and play with my dump truck."

"Doodle, we're almost there."

Palmer stops at the outskirts of the city only long enough to give Maggie a call, and then he follows her directions into town. Second exit off the freeway . . . you pass a lake and then you go along frat row, and when you see the campanile ahead you take a right . . . past the Skampburger and the E-Z-Freez.

There she is, standing like some southern belle under a live oak at the side of the road, just beyond the E-Z-Freez. Her suitcases are beside her, and she is so familiar . . . what, after all, has Palmer been expecting? Somehow he has been expecting a revelation. Somehow he has been expecting that his first sight of her will be something marvelous and strange. But there is nothing about her that is marvelous or strange, nothing at all.

"Jackie—who's that woman there?"

"Mama!" Jackie cries. "Mama!"—and he stands up on the seat and leans out the window with his arms spread wide, straining to embrace her even before the car comes to a stop.

"O my Jackie, how I've missed you!"

"I've missed you, mama!"

And for the little boy it has suddenly all become worth while—a trip of a thousand miles, on the red seat, surrounded by strangers: it has brought him to his mama! But for Palmer it is as though he is at the beginning of a journey and not a journey's end. It is as though she never left, it is as though they have lived in this landscape of verdure and decay all the days of their lives: she is as familiar, in this setting, as the neon logo of some gas station or motel or hamburger inn, replicated in ten thousand little towns across the country—you can't escape them though you drive a thousand miles, and in all those miles, too, he has never escaped from her.

She looks at him and he climbs out of the van, but he does not know what to do with her. He puts his arm around her; a small dry kiss is exchanged. She pulls away awkwardly and kneels to hug Jackie again, and Palmer throws her suitcases into the van. On top of one of the suitcases there are a couple of paperbacks.

"These aren't yours," he says. "Where is this great apartment you found?"

"I b-bought those. Can we get something to eat first?"

"It's getting late—we'll be needing some groceries anyway, won't we?"

"I guess. Poor Jackie, you look so tired! He looks like a little urchin," she tells Palmer. "Did you give him a bath at all since I left?"

"He's been rolling around in the dirt."

"*You're* still wearing the same shirt, I see."

*   *   *

They get to her apartment after dark. She opens her front door into the hot, stale air that is left over from midday. She tries all the switches but nothing works.

"Th-th-they *promised*."

"Take it easy."

"They *promised* to have the electricity on!" He fetches a flashlight for her and goes back to the van to get the gasoline lantern. In the sallow blue light from a carbonarc streetlamp across the way, the place looks like a motel. A row of gleaming bluish automobiles faces a row of gleaming bluish blond front doors across a narrow strip of bluish grass where three young crepe myrtles struggle to survive, and the three crepe myrtles, too, are blue.

He holds his lantern up and goes inside. The apartment has concrete walls. It has built-in carpeting, green, that flows from wall to wall and from one room into another.

"You know something, mama?"

"What, Jackie?"

"I missed you!"

"O, Jackie, I missed you, too! You must be hungry."

Palmer goes from room to room with his lantern. It's a big place, and the size of it is somehow painful to him. It has three bedrooms and two toilets and ten closets. The damn place—

why, the damn place is bigger than any place they've ever lived! Of course it costs more, too. But what does Maggie need with all that space? And the concrete walls make it feel a little like a crypt. He stands in front of one of the closets, just looking into it: the metal shelf, the metal bar—all this emptiness, dear god.

"What's the matter?" Maggie says from the doorway.

"Why do you need ten closets? What are you going to do with ten closets?"

"Isn't it absurd? You didn't see a roach in there or something, did you?"

"Nothing."

She has made Jackie a cheese sandwich, and he's lying on his side, on the sea of green carpeting, munching and munching—making believe his sandwich is a sailboat like the one he went on in the summer. Palmer brings in Jackie's own mattress from the van and Maggie covers it with a clean sheet.

"I hope you brought his babies."

"Sure."

When he brings in the little bear and the elephant with the pink vest, Maggie is showing Jackie what is going to be his room. The little boy is half asleep—talking to his mother from a dream:

"Where are we going to put up the tent?"

"We don't *have* to put up the tent—this is going to be our home. And this will be your room. You'll have your own room!"

"I don't want my own room."

"And your own toilet through that door—just like Yurii's room, where he used to live."

"Where's Yurii?"

"Don't know, Jackie. It's time for bed."

"I want a story."

"There's no time for that tonight."

"I want a back-rub."

Palmer leaves them alone and looks through the groceries they bought. He puts some of the things away and takes the rest nextdoor. He knocks. Then it occurs to him that he has not shaved or combed his hair in three days; his shorts are ragged and his shirt, which says Hog Protein in purple letters, is stained with grease—but it is too late to think of these things: he already hears footsteps inside. A young woman with short blond hair and a sleeveless pink dress opens the door. Her eyes bounce from his face to the items of food he is carrying, the hamburger, the milk, the eggs, and then she smiles.

"My word, for a moment ah thought you were Arty, coming to scare the daylights out of me!"

"No," says Palmer, "I'm—"

"Jamey, ah thought it was Arty!" she calls to someone inside—a plump twelve-year-old boy, Palmer sees, sunken into the velveteen couch and watching television.

"We just moved in next door," Palmer says, "and our refrigerator—"

"How nice! Come on inside heah."

He steps inside and grins at her stupidly. The boy glares at him from the couch. On the television a policeman has just been shot. "Who's going to tell his wife, chief?" another policeman asks. "That's what I want to know. Who's going to tell his wife?"

"Hi," Palmer says. "I'm Rob."

"And ah'm Mary Sue. So pleased to know you."

"Wondering if we could leave this stuff in your fridge overnight—our electricity isn't hooked up yet."

"Why, that's *terrible*! You set right down and let me pour you a cup of coffee!"

*   *   *

When he comes back to Maggie's apartment, it is dark. She has turned the lantern off; the only light is the pale light that comes through the window from the streetlamp outside.

"Maggie?" he whispers. There isn't any answer. He waits inside the door until his eyes adjust to the dark, and then he sees her. She has spread out the sleeping bags in the middle of the green carpet, and she seems to be asleep already. Palmer feels pretty tired too. He throws off his clothes and lies down beside her.

But suddenly she sits up and stares at him wide-eyed, as though frightened.

"O! Who is it? O! O!"

And what is that outfit she is wearing? Old gray rags, stitched together—she looks like the little match girl, but her rags have been arranged so that one breast is bare and one thigh is uncovered all the way up to the symphisis pubis.

"Hwat are yew doing in my bed? Plize don't 'urt me, sir!"

Perhaps her accent is supposed to be that of a cockney streetgirl of a hundred years ago.

"You wouldn't dew me no 'arm now, wouldjou?"

"You want me to fuck you?" Palmer says.

Maggie pulls the rags around her a little closer and leans toward him.

"Oi don't think you mean me no 'arm—*you* wouldn't 'urt me, sir, *would*jou? Nao—of *course* you wouldn't!"

He feels her warm breath against his skin, and he closes his eyes. The smell of gasoline is still in the air from the lantern, and dust that must come from those rags she is wearing, and a smell that is the smell of a woman.

"Hwat's this now—no britches?"

"God," he whispers. "God."

*   *   *

At the end of the room, back of the long green drapes, there are sliding glass doors, and when you push the drapes aside a little you see a kempt green lawn—and beyond, on the other side of the blacktop road, the trees, the great fat dark loose-jowled live oaks, scattered through low-lying fields of brown waist-high grass and weeds and reeds: it is a savanna, it is like Africa: you expect to see baboons, you expect to see the lion and the hyena and some great vulture setting down to bury her head in the wildebeest's rosy guts.

Maggie looks at him sleepily from the nest of sheets and sleeping bags in the middle of the carpet.

"What time is it?"

"It's early," he whispers. "Go back to sleep."

"But what *time* is it?"

"Quarter to six."

"Qu-quarter to *six*?"

Maggie pulls one of the sleeping bags over her head angrily. Palmer goes out. He walks around the building through the dewy grass and then sits in the front seat of the van, looking at the row of blond front doors and the windows and the three crepe myrtle trees and the narrow strip of grass. His mother's letter is still in his pocket.

We were so happy to have had you all here a year ago. I don't know what has been the outstanding feature of this summer—our two days at the Cliffs in July, Laura's dogs stay with us in Aug. (!), my painting of D. B. a couple of weeks ago. The latter actually was a good time as I spent a night out there. Rose came out the next afternoon to pick me up and I had a lovely dinner with them out on their cool verdant porch. (I stress the "cool" because it was hot weather.) Then Kenny motored me home.

One morning on the radio the "good music station" played Gottschalk's *Tarantella* and it was a real invigorator—One's feet tapped and one was suddenly energized! Are you aware of it? I wonder if you have such a thing as a "good music station" out there.

No more news to report, but now that I have Maggie's address I'll write her a word of cheer, because I'm sure she misses having her man around and may be lonely even when little Jackie comes down to fill the void. I hope all is well and happy for her—and you—and darling little Jackie— Blessings abundant on you all three.

People are beginning to come out of the blond doors and drive away. In one of the windows Jackie's face suddenly appears. Palmer waves at him, and in a moment he comes running out the door in his underpants.

"Daddy, don't go! I want to kiss you good-bye!"

"I'm not going yet, doodle—I'm just sitting here."

"Why?"

"I don't know . . . Because it's such a nice morning. Don't you think it's a nice morning?"

*   *   *

Dear mama. It was so good of you to write. I do not believe that Maggie is going to miss "having her man around." What does it mean, having her man around? It means nothing, nothing for months on end but trivialities, nothing but the day-to-day occurrences of breathing, eating, sleeping, and getting in each other's way. How can I tell you anything of my relationship with Maggie, mama? . . . Yet some days it all seems beautiful, it all seems to make sense, everything seems to fall into place . . .

*   *   *

He drives Maggie to the campus. She's early for her classes, and Palmer suggests that he and Jackie might come inside and wait with her awhile.

"You can show us that famous three-way stage."

She answers with a moment's silence. ". . . Some other time, maybe." She kisses Jackie and turns away.

Palmer drives with Jackie into the center of town. It is a beautiful city. It is an old city and it is full of greenery, full of the fertile bosoms of plants pressed up to the moist, sun-filled air. There are magnolias, and there are live oaks draped with spanish moss, and there are palms and palmettos, and there are a thousand other plants, growing and growing and growing. In a glass building surrounded by magnolias a woman with pink cotton-candy hair promises to have the electricity turned on.

"Y'all have any more trouble, you just give us a call, you hear?"

Then Palmer drives to another section of town to look for the thrift stores and secondhand shops. There are narrow, dirty streets, and rows of ramshackle houses supported on cinderblocks and roofed with corrugated sheets of zinc. This is where people kill each other with knives on Saturday nights, and this is where they get together and sing the blues. And the sun beats down over all, and even from the cracks in the pavement great leafy weeds arise.

Everything in the shops looks like garbage. In one place Palmer finally sees a chest of drawers and a couch that might be okay, but he is so weary from looking over all the discards and all the stained, smelly remnants of other people's lives that he cannot bring himself to buy anything.

"Let's go, doodle."

"Daddy, I'm thirsty."

Outside, the slum street is hot and mostly deserted, but there are three coffee-colored teenagers, two with cream and one without, lounging against a bent, rusty wire fence across the sidewalk from Palmer's van. They regard him silently, impassively, through half-shut lids. Palmer does not look at them. They are just kids of twelve or thirteen, but nowadays a lot of these kids carry knives or razor blades.

"Let's see if we can find you a place to get something to drink, Jackie, and then we'll go pick up Maggie—and you're probably hungry, too!—and then we can go see what your new day-care is going to be like. What do you think?"

But Jackie does not say anything. While Palmer is unlocking the van, Jackie just stands there beside him and glares at the three kids.

"Shi-i-it," he says suddenly, and Palmer gives him a swift slap on the arm—much too hard.

"God damn it, doodle, just keep your goddamn mouth shut!"

He picks Jackie up and thrusts him into the van, and then climbs in beside him. Jackie is indignant and petulant. "I want to get in by myself!" Two of the kids on the sidewalk are laughing, laughing so freely and so hysterically that Palmer would feel inclined to laugh with them were it not for Jackie. The third kid is still staring at Palmer with half-closed eyes.

"You *hurted* me," Jackie says, his lip quivering, as Palmer drives away.

"I'm sorry, doodle—I'm really sorry, but you know better than to say that. People don't like to hear that—things like that. They take it as an insult."

He drives on for a few blocks, out of the slums, heading back toward the campus, but Jackie is still pouting.

"You hurted my feelings!"

"O doodle—" Palmer pulls the van over to the side of the road and gives his son a hug. "I think you're all right. Let's go get an ice-cream cone, and then we can pick up Maggie."

*   *   *

Maggie found a day-care center, but she is not entirely happy with it. It's at a church nearby, and Palmer drives her and Jackie over. The children are cared for by nuns.

"What are you supposed to call them?" Palmer says as they get out of the van. "Do you call them mother?"

"Sister!" Maggie whispers.

"But the men are called father, isn't that right?"

"I'm not sure."

The children and the nuns are in a fenced-in play area behind the church. There are three nuns, and they are full of joy. The children, too, are not unhappy, but Jackie ignores all the children and goes from one piece of playground equipment to another—the small slide, the big slide, the swings, the tunnel made of drainpipes, the jungle-gym, and the big slide once again—and tries them all out.

"It's depressing," Palmer whispers to Maggie.

"What do you mean?"

"Everything is so clean."

One of the nuns comes over and Maggie talks to her while Palmer looks at the children. Here they do not get together and giggle about shit and poop, as they did at Jackie's old day-care. Here you do not see them wandering around naked. Here they are all combed and scrubbed, and there is not a single one of them who is shirtless and barefoot, as Jackie has been since the last frost in April. But the nun is telling Maggie that there are regulations. Jackie may stay today, but in the future the regulations will have to be "enfo'ced."

She takes Maggie and Palmer on a tour of the classrooms. Maggie has been through it before, and as they walk down the hallway she and the nun are talking together like old friends. Why should this be so amazing to Palmer? In a few minutes he figures it out—Maggie isn't stuttering.

They return to the playground, where Jackie is telling another little boy that he is Batman. "And Yurii is Robin. You don't know Yurii—he moved away."

"Ready to go, doodle?" Palmer says.

"I'm playing—I don't want to go."

"We may not be back for several hours."

"I want to *stay*," Jackie says.

Palmer and Maggie go back to the van.

"It doesn't seem as though we should leave him here on his first day in Louisiana," he says, starting the engine.

"He'll be okay. Did you find any furniture?"

"I don't know—I don't know if it was all junk."

"I *need* some furniture."

"You don't stutter any more, do you?" Palmer says. He smiles at her, but Maggie just gives him a strange look and sits there without answering. "I'm sorry," he says. "You're still sensitive about it."

"I'm not sensitive," she says. "But I haven't stuttered for at least five years. Let's go take a look at the furniture."

*   *   *

She likes the things he found—the old couch, the chest of drawers. They are absolutely beautiful. They are like the furniture she used to see in the home of some neighbor in the little Boston suburb where she grew up: things that had character and grace and charm, unlike the furniture her parents had. She loves these things! Palmer sees them now with different eyes; to him too they now seem like real finds. How is it that he allowed himself to pass out of this shop a couple of hours ago with only a feeling of disgust? Maggie is looking over the piles of junk with eyes bright with discovery. She finds something more, an old wobbly picnic table with a couple of benches, festooned with cobwebs, which she thinks she can use as a dining table or a desk or—well, something. The mountainous, bushy-browed woman at the cash register, sitting so the fan sends breezes up between her thighs, shouts to someone in the back of the store, and a slender twenty-year-old with marceled hair and a pencil-line mustache, who is perhaps Mexican or perhaps a mixture of all the peoples of the world, appears through the faded rose curtains and helps Palmer and Maggie with the couch. Trying to lift it is like trying to lift a car.

"Shit," Palmer says.

"Gah damn, man," says the little guy. There is a stench of

perfume or pomade about him. He and Maggie are laboring at one end of the couch, Palmer at the other.

"It's a hide-a-bed, that's what it is," the woman says. She gets off her stool and comes over. "See?" She throws the cushions onto the floor, reaches in back, and opens the couch into a bed. The mattress has a charred hole, big enough to fall through, in its center—it's not any good for sleeping on any more, but all the metal is still there, half a ton of iron braces and levers and cross-pieces and springs. The woman pokes at the edges of the hole with her finger. "Smoking in bed. Tst tst."

She goes back to her stool and rests her elbows on the glass countertop as the three of them shove and drag the couch out onto the sidewalk. The little guy is not much help in getting it into the van; he is lifting with one hand and holding the other hand to the small of his back.

"O, my hernorrhoids!"

He sits down on the dirty step leading into the shop, still holding his back, while Palmer and Maggie carry out the other things by themselves. He smiles up at them, candidly and apologetically, every time they go past; his teeth gleam; he rubs his back. When Maggie and Palmer are through and they are climbing into the van, he stands up again and grins with gleaming teeth and waves his arms to catch their attention.

"That thing give me a hernorrhoid!" he yells, patting his back. "A hernorrhoid, man!"

*   *   *

They unload the furniture at Maggie's apartment. It does not do a very good job of filling three bedrooms and a living room, but at least they have something to sit on while they drink their coffee. Palmer's back aches too and he thinks that perhaps he was right in the first place and there was no reason to buy this goddamned piece of furniture. The couch has many odors that were not apparent before they began sitting on it: dust and must and the smell of charred fiber (or is that only his imagination?) and a definite reek of cat urine. Maggie is a little tense; Palmer can see that she is just waiting for him to begin criticizing *her* choice of furniture so that she can remind him that first of all it was *his* choice of furniture and that if he did not like it, he had a mouth, didn't he? and he could have told her in the store that he did not like it, and anyway it is *her* furniture, hers and Jackie's, and it is *her* apartment, and *she* is the one who is going to be living here, and *she* is the one who is going to be sitting on this couch (which *she* likes), and not Palmer!

"Thanks for the coffee," he says.

"You didn't care for that place, did you?" She sits down on one of the wobbly wooden benches.

"It was okay—I just didn't expect the couch to weigh so much."

"I mean the day-care."

"I don't know anything about nuns."

"I don't think they'll make him into a religious freak."

"Maybe someplace else would be better," he says.

"I looked at a lot of places."

She has a mimeographed list of nurseries and day-care centers. Palmer gets himself another cup of coffee and looks it over. Beside each name she has put little pencil marks—dashes and checks and crosses and stars and dollar signs and "t f," which means "too far."

"I don't want to spend half the day taking him every-where," she says.

She moves onto the couch beside him and watches him going down the list.

"What about this place—this Humphrey Dumpty? It sounds pretty good. Gymnastics . . . art instruction . . . gateway to kindergarten."

"Too expensive," she says.

"I'll send you the extra money."

Palmer can feel how uncomfortable this false, extravagant promise makes her. They are both silent for a moment.

"The money isn't important," she says.

"What the hell is a gateway to kindergarten? What a terrible name the place has! Disgusting!"

Maggie gets up and tosses her coffee down the drain. "Go ahead and look the place over," she says. "I want him to be in a place where he's happy."

*   *   *

It is four converted houses, joined by a covered walkway and surrounded by a chain-link fence. In front of the fence is a sign with cabbage-green letters about the height of a four-year-old child and with a depiction of two egglike creatures with spindly arms and legs. One is wearing spats and a top hat, the other a pink gown. Both are grinning grotesquely.

Palmer looks at them a moment, then goes through the gate. There are tricycles and swings and a slide and all the other paraphernalia, but still the play area looks like a dog run. He can hear muffled children's voices from the houses, and suddenly the wail of an infant. Each of the houses has its own sign: Tiny Tots, Tom Thumbs, Three Bears, and Giant-Killers. The main office is in Three Bears and the baby is crying in Tiny Tots. As Palmer walks past the swings, he hears a woman's voice:

"Keep that up and I'll give you something to cry about!"

Palmer lets himself into the office. Except for the lamp on the desk it is dark. It is walled in dark wood paneling, like a funeral home, and there is a thick white carpet on the floor. In a moment the plump woman behind the desk looks up at him.

"How can we be of service to you today?"

"Looking for a day-care," Palmer says. "For my son."

She's wearing a formal black dress that looks as though it came from Paris, but she reeks of perfume like a whore. Her hair is silvery and it is garlanded in fat curls around her face. Her cheeks are powdered pink.

"Fill out one of these applications, please."

Her knackwurst fingers shine with a dozen oversized rings as she hands him the pen from her ebony desk-set. The desk is made of some rich, heavy, gleaming wood, like a banker's desk. She flutters a bangled wrist insouciantly backwards.

"These . . . are some of our little ones," she says. There are a few framed studio photos of children on the wall. Palmer glances at the photos and then picks up the application. He goes through it dubiously while she asks questions about his "line of work" and about his "place of residence" and about his "expectations for the future."

"We're not transients," he says.

"Sir, I'm sure you're not. And how old is the child in question?"

"He'll be four."

"Very good . . ." She presses a buzzer on her desk and she pulls a black leather notebook from one of the desk drawers. She opens the notebook seemingly at random and makes some sort of mark in it. "Then he'll be a Giant-Killer." Resting the cap of her pen against her lower lip, she keeps looking at the open page until the door opens and a young mulatto woman in a bright multicolored dress, white and red and green, comes in. "Miss Naboo, this is Mister Palmer, and his son would like to be a Giant-Killer."

"First or second class?"

"Second class."

"Very well, then I'll show him our facilities."

Palmer follows her around, from room to room, from one house to the next. Here is the dining area, with a mural of monkeys and tigers and elephants and palm trees, and with tables that fold down from the walls; in the closet over there are the gymnastic mats—Miss Naboo opens the door and points them out.

"And once a week we are privileged to have the services of a modern dance teacher."

Here is the room where movies are shown to the older children, here is the art room, here are the three-year-olds—Miss Naboo stands there in the doorway a moment, smiling benignantly at the three-year-olds, who are playing with cups and kitchen implements in a raised sandbox. In the backyard there are some other three-year-olds, sitting around two metal picnic tables and eating pieces of chocolate cake—it is someone's birthday.

"These are the Three Bears first-classes," Miss Naboo explains.

They look happy, all right. Palmer smiles. A little girl with straight black hair catches his eye and crams an entire piece of cake into her mouth; her cheeks bulge and then she giggles, spluttering a cannonade of crumbs. Miss Naboo is heading onwards; with her hand on the doorknob of the Giant-Killers' house, she waits for Palmer to come along.

"Now here are the older four-year-olds, the Giant-Killers first-class. Let me show you some of their workbooks."

"They have workbooks?"

"We've found that they are decidedly beneficial in starting the child off on the right foot."

She plucks a workbook off a shelf, opens it, and holds it out to Palmer. "This is by one of our better students." A capital letter is printed at the top of the page and then there are a series of parallel blue lines on which somebody has penciled the same letter again and again all the way to the bottom of the page.

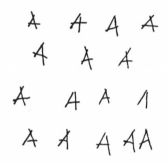

Palmer keeps looking at the page and it makes him feel unaccountably depressed. Miss Naboo waits in silence. In a minute Palmer hands back the workbook.

"Jackie doesn't know how to write," he confesses.

"Many of the Giant-Killer second-classes do not have that facility yet. That's why we have these," says Miss Naboo, patting the pile of workbooks. "We like to think that at Humphrey Dumpty we are encouraging our children to take their first tentative steps down the long arduous road toward adulthood."

She smiles at Palmer. Palmer smiles back at her, and tells her that before he can sign Jackie up definitely he will have to talk over one or two things with his wife, but he is certainly impressed with the place.

"It is certainly," he says, still smiling at her, "it is certainly . . . an impressive place."

*   *   *

"How was it?" she asks when he comes in. "Was it any good? You were right—I should have checked that place out before. The money isn't important—maybe it isn't good having him around those nuns."

Palmer walks past her and opens the refrigerator.

"What happened to that beer?"

"It's in the back there—see it?"

He opens a can of beer and stands in the small kitchen drinking it. Outside the kitchen window he can see his van and he can see the other cars parked in the lot and he can see the grease spots shimmering on the concrete in the sunlight and the pink flowers of one of the crepe myrtle trees that grow on the narrow strip of grass. And Maggie is still there behind him, waiting at the counter that divides the kitchen from the living room—why won't she go away? He finishes the beer and crushes the can.

"I don't feel like talking about it," he says.

"Why? Was it that bad? Wh-what was wrong with it?"

He gets himself another beer and he looks at the wall instead of her as he goes past and he sits on the couch and drinks his beer. And there is a voice in his mind that keeps saying: P-p-please keep your g-g-g-goddamn mouth shut—p-p-p-please d-d-do that for me.

She is quiet for a long time. When he gets up to throw the second beer can away, he sees that she is not there. She has disappeared into one of the bedrooms. He finds her sitting on the floor, on the green carpet, with her arms around her shins and her knees up to pillow her head.

"It's about time to pick up Jackie," he says.

"I know." She doesn't look up.

"Are you going to come?"

"Yes."

"Then let's go."

"Okay."

But her face remains hidden against her knees. Palmer goes out and waits for her in the van. In a few minutes she comes out too and climbs in without looking at him.

But when he starts the engine, she bursts out angrily:

"You never *talk*!"

"The nuns are okay," Palmer says. "The nuns are pretty good."

"But why can't you talk about it! Why can't you just *say* if you didn't like the place!"

"I just think he's better where he is," Palmer says. And they do not talk about it any more.

*   *   *

The children are out in the play yard behind the church, and two nuns sit side by side on a wooden bench, smiling as though they are beholding here, amid the sunshine and the babble of children's voices, some unanswerable epiphany of the human spirit. Palmer can hear Jackie's loud bright laughter above all the other sounds of the playground, and in a moment he sees him: he is upside-down beneath the slide, hanging by toes and fingers like a sloth. There are two other little boys standing on the ground beside Jackie, watching with what appears to be awe and incredulity. When Maggie calls his name, Jackie drops to the ground and comes running over, talking already, already telling her, before he comes to a halt, about the marvelous things he has done in this place—a movie with a monkey in it, mama! a monkey named George! and they have been finger-painting! and they had a snack! and it was crackers and milk!

"But what happened to your shirt, Jackie?" Maggie says— his T-shirt is ripped all the way across the front so that there is a great flap that hangs down to his knees.

"I tried to put my foot in it, mama! This is my new friend—" He turns and looks at the two little boys, who have followed him over and are standing there eyeing him shyly.

"But Jackie—why would you put your foot in your shirt?"

"*I* don't know. These are my new friends, mama," Jackie says. "Can we go home now?"

*   *   *

Dear mama. I do not like to hurt you, but I think it's time to tell the truth. Maggie and I are not in love. We have never been in love. I met her at a cast party when we were at the university and all I wanted to do was sleep with her. I felt sorry for her because she stuttered. I didn't know she was an actress. I told her I hated the theater, I thought it was phony, I thought all the actors were phonies—I was just saying what I thought she wanted to hear, and Maggie thought I was a part of the Real World. I didn't know she was the leading lady until someone else tried to tell me so several weeks later; I told him he was crazy.

Mama, we should never have been together for even one single day. All I wanted was someone to sleep with. All she wanted . . . I don't know what she wanted, but there wasn't anything that should have kept us together.

How did it happen that we brought forth a child? How does it happen that we've been together for ten years? How did all these things happen, mama, when we never even fell in love?

*   *   *

When Palmer begins to unload the things he packed beneath the platform in the back of the van—Maggie's clothes and Maggie's bike and the vacuum cleaner and the stereo and the television and all of Jackie's toys—he finds a pair of black cowboy boots with rhinestones, wedged in behind the front seat. He brings them in to Maggie.

"Can you use these?"

She takes the boots, looks at them, sniffs at them—they still give off the good rich smell of new leather—but then gives Palmer a look of astonishment.

"What size do you think my feet are? These must belong to a midget!"

"*I* want them," Jackie says.

"You're not a midget, doodle."

"Anyway I don't think I look good in cowboy boots . . ."

"Those are *mine*," Jackie says.

Jackie sits on the kitchen floor and pulls the boots on, and all evening, while they are driving from one shopping center to another through the Louisiana night that is so black and thick

and summery and so suffused with the heavy sweet smells of
flowers and decay, all evening, while they are looking in all the
shopping centers for all the little things that Maggie needs, the
wastebaskets and the dishdrainers and the shower curtains
and the soap dishes and all the interminable things that Maggie needs, all evening he wears the boots and says he is a cowboy, and when they get home and it is time for him to go to bed
he wants to wear his boots to bed, but Maggie says he may *not*
wear his boots to bed.

"But mama—"

"You are not going to wear those boots to bed!"

"I want to tell you something!"

"I don't care what you tell me, you're not wearing boots to
bed!"

So Jackie takes off his boots and cuddles them like babies,
together with his elephant and his bear with the green bow tie.

"Aunt Berry gave me these, right, daddy?"

"I guess so, doodle."

"Who is Aunt *Berry*?"

Maggie kisses the little boy goodnight, and Palmer kisses
him goodnight, and Maggie kisses the elephant and the bear,
and in a little while, when all the sounds from Jackie's bedroom
have ceased, Palmer looks up from the couch to see Maggie
standing in the doorway to one of the bedrooms. She is a nurse
in a white uniform, but the white uniform is unbuttoned halfway down the front, and her hand is on her hip, and when she
sees she has gotten Palmer's full attention she sidles toward
him with her hips moving back and forth like a small boat lost
on the tempestuous waves of the sea.

"Now Mistah Palmah, ah sweah to goodness ah hope you
are feeling betteh afteh thet ope*ra*tion of youahs. Now ah just
want to dim these here *lahts* a little, Mistah Palmah, and—let
me see, Mistah Palmah, do you think you can give me a little
smile?—and ah think ah would lahk to examine youah wound
a little more closely now, and maybe cleanse it off a little. Mistah Palmah, did you know that the very best antiseptic known
to man is human saliva?—that's *raht*, Mistah Palmah, human
saliva—and ah got plenty of that raht here in mah own little

mouth . . . Is *that* wheah youah wound is, Mistah Palmah? Is *that* wheah it is?"

*   *   *

In the middle of the night, when they both find themselves awake at the same time (did Jackie cry out in his sleep?), Maggie tells Palmer she needs a bed. She's got to have a bed—he can't go back north until she has a bed. It's impossible to get any rest on this concrete floor, and how is she supposed to teach and take care of Jackie all day if she can't get to sleep all night?

"Okay."

"I mean it—I need a bed."

"Okay, let's get a bed."

"I can see you care a lot about it!"

And she turns her back on him angrily. But when she wakes up beside him in the morning, she is unexpectedly tender. She does something she has not done in a long time—probably never. She takes his hand in both of hers and she looks at it and she kisses it and she runs her fingertips across it, as though she has only just now, after ten years, discovered this amazing appendage of his. The tenderness is so extraordinary that Palmer does not know what to do with it. He feels like laughing—god, it is such a joke! At the same time his other hand, under the sleeping bag, is clenched so tightly that his fingernails bite into the skin of his palm, and there is a terrible knot in his stomach. In a moment he has to close his eyes. God damn you! he thinks. God damn your god damned actors' exercises! God damn your tactile manipulations! God damn your damned digital sensitivities! God damn every god damned phony trick that makes you come alive whenever you're on a stage!

In a minute she lets go of his hand and he opens his eyes.

"I was thinking," she says. "Maybe the thing is that our sexual relationship wasn't working out so well because we were just never getting to bed at the same time."

"Maybe it's just that I'm a shit."

"No, I'm serious."

"Well, maybe that's right," Palmer says.

Maggie pulls on a pair of black tights and a red skirt and heads into the kitchen.

"I guess we should have thought about that earlier," she says.

In a minute she comes back with two cups of coffee.

"One of the girls has an old bed she said we can have," she says offhandedly. "She's the set-designer. But . . ."

"Why don't we go get it?"

"She says it's pretty old."

"It can't be that bad," Palmer says.

"She lives pretty far out—she has a horse ranch."

"We can go out there tonight. It won't hurt us to look at it."

*   *   *

There is nothing, where they leave the highway, that looks like horse country. The vegetation is sparse, the soil is sandy. Here and there they see trailers, with German shepherds chained to the front doors. There are road signs and uncompleted roads—roads that lead to dead ends and roads that lead to deserted circles and roads that drop off suddenly into the sand. A sign at the side of the road says "Enchantment Acres"—it looks like a subdivision someone had hopes for twenty years ago, and then forgot.

"This is the right place," Maggie says. "Now we look for Serendipity Drive."

Palmer turns down Serendipity Drive. A few more trailers . . . some kids playing on a junked car with a smashed windshield and with all its tires gone . . . a smell of burning rubber.

"Now the first left," Maggie says. "Wait—was that a street?"

Palmer backs up and they look at the sign.

"That's it," she says. "Huey P. Long Court. O God—that must be the place over there. I see a horse."

There's a stable, a trailer, a couple of wooden outbuildings. Palmer drives the van under a sign whose letters, carved out of wood, stand out against the sky: "Rancho Bar-None." A woman with chestnut hair and flaring nostrils is waiting for them at the door of the trailer.

"Why Maggie-Sue, these must be the two men in your life! Hi, you all, I'm Flozelle, and I want you to come in and meet my old mammy!"

"When are we going to see the horses?" Jackie whispers, clutching Maggie's hand.

"Just be patient."

Inside the trailer Flozelle introduces them to her mother, a little woman like a dumpling—round and shapeless and with a doughy complexion.

"I'll go pour some soda for the little boy," she says.

"Now mama, you've been drinking an awful lot of soda today."

"It's not for me, it's for the little boy! *You'd* like some soda, wouldn't you, darling?"

Jackie nods shyly. She brings a glass of fizzy brown liquid out to him, and he sits on the couch next to Maggie with the glass in his hand. On the wall above the couch there are some paintings of horses. Jackie looks down into the liquid but he does not drink it.

"How do you like my paintings, Mister Palmer?" Flozelle says.

"They're *nice.*" Palmer walks around the room, stopping briefly in front of each painting. *"Nice."* The paintings are of different sizes, but they are all portraits of horses—a head, a massive neck, and a monochrome background of red or green or navy blue. One of the horses is eating a carrot. One has a tear in its eye. "You're quite an artist," Palmer says.

"Jackie, do you like jokes?" Flozelle's mother says.

"O mama—" Flozelle winks at Maggie.

"I'm going to tell you a joke. Once there was a little girl who was just about your age, maybe a little older. She was five or six. Well, one day her mother had company, and the company said: My, but little Susie—the little girl's name was Susie—*my,* but little Susie is P. R. E. T. T. Y. Well, then the mother turned to her guest and said: Little Susie is not only P. R. E. T. T. Y., she's also S. M. A. R. T.!"

Palmer is still waiting for the punch line. Flozelle throws both hands up to her forehead and Maggie gives a polite little laugh, but Jackie laughs so hard that tears come to his eyes.

"Really, mama," Flozelle says. "Well, you all, now that you've come all the way out here to visit us I'd like to show you some of our horses."

"Ooo—Jackie would *love* that," Maggie says.

"How about it, Jackie?" says Flozelle. "You think you'd like to come out and see some fine old horses?"

Jackie just looks at her and clings to Maggie's hand.

"Jackie loves horses," Maggie says, "but he's pretending to be shy."

Flozelle leads them out to the stable and walks with them down the hay-covered aisle between the stalls. There are twenty or thirty horses. Flozelle talks to them like old friends; she whispers endearments and she rubs their noses. Here is one with a bandaged leg, poor dear; here is one who is too wild for his own good; here is one they have had for years and years—he's a regular member of the family; and this sorrel here, Flozelle says, is the most gentle horse she's ever met.

"You're a regular sweetheart, aren't you, dear?" she says, rubbing the horse's nose. "Would you like to get on her, Jackie?"

But Jackie is still hanging on to Maggie's hand, and he shakes his head no.

"It'd be fun, doodle," Palmer says.

"Mama will stand right beside you and hold you up there," Flozelle says. "She's a real sweet horse."

Jackie shakes his head again. "I don't *want* to."

"Well," Maggie says apologetically, as they walk out the other end of the stable, "I bet the next time we come out here he'll want to get on."

"You won't be able to keep him off!"

They follow Flozelle across a field, some sort of training field where horses' hooves have worn a circular path in the earth, and then they have to crawl under a barbwire fence.

"Now, I hope this bed is going to be okay, Maggie—you know I wouldn't want to have you all out here on a wild goose chase!"

They cross a ravine and come to an old shack. It is open on one side and it is filled with an assortment of junk. An Irish setter gets up from the mattress and wags his tail wildly as he bats his nose against Flozelle's thigh.

"You old thing! So this is where you've been, you old thing! Well, that mattress sure doesn't look like much."

There are three televisions and a clothes-dryer, an automobile radiator, an old trunk. The mattress is faded from the sun and stained from the rain—maybe the dog has been pissing on it, too, or giving birth to litters of puppies.

"Maggie, I feel just awful! Brought you all the way out here and this mattress is just terrible!"

"Well—"

"I haven't even been over here to look at things since April! I had no idea!"

"Well, it isn't that bad," Maggie says.

"Maggie, I can't let you take home an old piece of junk like that to sleep on!"

"Flozelle, it's okay," Maggie says. "It's just a little faded, that's all . . . But it's okay."

*   *   *

All the way home they can smell the mattress in the back of the van. It smells like wet hay and like horses. Maggie does not say anything about the mattress, but Palmer knows she will not sleep on a mattress like that. They have had some pretty bad mattresses. They have lived in lousy places, in terrible places, in rotten little one-room places where they did not even have a mattress. In San Francisco they slept on ninety-nine cent plastic air-mattresses for eight months, and in other places they have slept on other mattresses, on ripped, filthy mattresses, on mattresses with the stuffing coming out, on mattresses stained with blood and with coffee and with scotch and with semen. But Palmer knows, without Maggie's saying so, that Maggie cannot sleep on this mattress. This mattress is not for her, not now, not in this new apartment where two toilets beckon and ten closets stand with open doors and all that fine thick carpeting stretches like a green sea from wall to wall to wall. No: the mattress is only a memory of the hard times, it is only a memory of their past, and now the times have ceased to be hard—now the times will not be hard for her any more and he will go back north and find a new woman, he will go up north and she will stay here and start her new life, la vita nuova, a life that will not be hard, a life that will be as smooth and as warm as the breeze that comes through the September night up from the Gulf: and this mattress will not do because she will have men in, men of every description, men of every race, creed, and color, but mostly men who will remind her, in some way, of him (but they will be kinder, and they will be more patient, and they will have sleek lean bodies like panthers), and she will be ashamed of this mattress, and she will be ashamed of everything there is that reminds her of the past . . .

He pulls up in the parking space in front of the crepe myrtles, and for a moment all of them just sit there, Palmer and Maggie and Jackie—Jackie has fallen asleep. Then Palmer gets out and tackles the mattress.

"Well, you won't be needing this," he says. He hauls it off to the trash bin while Maggie carries Jackie in to his bed. When he comes inside she has already pulled off the little boy's rhinestone boots and she has buried his elephant and his baby bear under the covers beside him. And Jackie is fast asleep, but she is kneeling by his bed, rubbing his back softly and slowly and whispering softly something about Wynken and Blynken and Nod.

*   *   *

In the morning he drives her again to the big discount department stores that sprawl across the shopping plazas that dot the southern universe like raisins in a bowl of hominy, and then they drive into the center of town and they wind up at a furniture store where the wood shines and curves like beautiful brown pottery. And she spends all of her first two weeks' paycheck, a munificent sum that once would have kept them alive for months, on a bed with five whorled knobs leaping up like dream dancers at its head and five little knobs crouched at its foot like pudgy cherubim in prayer. It has a mattress that is supposed to give you just the right amount of support, but not too much—to support you where you need to be supported, but everywhere else to let you float, somewhere in the great sea of dreams—and to actually give you more sleep in fewer hours (as proven in actual case studies at a well-known university of some repute) than an ordinary person would ordinarily get in a full night's sleep on an ordinary mattress. And a precision-engineered box spring so superbly constructed that you can jump up and down on one part of it while the springs in all the rest of it remain so stable that you can set a glass of water there, or blood, or scotch, or sperm, and it will remain unshaken and unspilled forever.

Well, Maggie is happy. And within hours the deliverymen bring the bed to her apartment. They haul it in in pieces, inside big cardboard boxes, and when they have put all the pieces together they haul all the boxes out empty.

"You're all set, old buddy," the foreman says to Palmer. "Pleasant dreams."

And then Maggie has everything she needs, everything a human being requires to exist in the deep south, but she and Palmer go out again anyway to buy some more. They go out to all the big stores at all the big shopping centers, and they stop by garage sales on the way home, and they come back with plants and decorations, with mirrors and with rugs for the bathrooms, with toiletbowl brushes and plastic flowerpots—it is a holy ritual, all this buying, it is like a rite of passage—they come back with a blue glass vase and with a piece of African material to hang on the wall, and finally with a mobile of glittering fish that will swim in the air over Jackie's bed like magic exhalations of his dreams. There is so much stuff . . . And there are other things, too, all those other things, all those photographs and drawings and all those other little decorative objects and mementos that Palmer carried south with him, packed beneath the platform in the van and packed among Maggie's clothes in trunks and in suitcases and in cardboard boxes—all those clanging camel bells and elephant bells and bells made of pottery, and the Wedgwood pitcher with its chipped lip, and the wind chimes of bamboo and of tinkling pink shell, and the antique mirror, and the African figurines with wooden faces lean and dark. Palmer brings all these things together; he hangs them on the walls and sets them on shelves, and tries to give a personality to Maggie's place. Maggie sits on the couch, reading plays and drinking gin and orange juice.

"Maybe the couch would be better against that wall," Palmer says. "What do you think?"

"I trust your judgment."

"Maggie, you said you wanted to do things on your own—remember? That was one of the reasons you wanted to get away—to have things your own way."

"I've got to get this done," she says, holding up her book. "You know about couches and things."

Palmer pours himself some gin and orange juice and thinks about where to put the figurines. So many of these things are *his* things—*he* has bought them or made them or found them—and he is putting them up in *his* way, but the place is not his, it is Maggie's, and Palmer rides the gin and orange juice like an inland waterway: it takes him here again, it takes him back to this apartment a month from now, or two months, or three, or five months from now, when the gentleman caller is coming through the door and the baby-sitter is being dismissed and the gentleman caller is taking off his overcoat and loosening his tie, and while Maggie disappears into the bathroom to do something with the little blue plastic case she keeps in the medicine cabinet the gentleman caller looks at the pictures, the photographs, the figurines, and the elephant bells and the camel bells and the wind chimes made of shell, and when Maggie comes out again the gentleman caller insists on looking in on little Jackie: he stands there a moment, smiling down on Maggie's son, and when they come out again and close the door to Jackie's room the gentleman caller says, almost with a catch in his voice, "My God, he's—he's beautiful! He looks so much like you, Maggie." Yes, Palmer thinks; when I am gone even my son will not be my own, but simply an aspect of Maggie's personality, an aspect of Maggie's scheme of interior decoration, an aspect of this circle that goes on and on: and all this interior decoration will go on and on, the coupling of moths and junebugs, crickets and cicadas, teddy bears and elephants, and even the coupling, Palmer thinks, even the coupling of human beings in complicated circumstances, filled with gin and orange juice, under the great wing of heaven.

"It's almost time to pick up Jackie," Maggie says. "O, I forgot to tell you—there's a letter from your mother."

"For me?"

"No, for me."

"What does she have to say?"

"Same old stuff. Here—read it yourself." She gets up to make herself a salad, then sits on the arm of the couch, watching him read the letter, while she eats it.

Dear Maggie,

I hope you are finding life fruitful and rewarding in your new locale. I imagine a fractured family condition cannot help but bring some degree of loneliness. But when two careers are concerned there would seem to be no alternative. I suppose life is never simple. But I have a feeling that whatever happens is for our good if only we use the experience to turn to our advantage constructively and expectantly.

A career, especially a supportive one, can't be gainsaid. Life is sometimes a real ache-in-the-heart for mortal man (or woman) and it is then that the creative spirit can alleviate by giving voice or vision in a golden outpouring so that others may share. I am confident that your creative fields will mesh again when the goals at hand are accomplished. One has to be true to the determination to live "not *somehow,* but *triumphantly.*" Dear Maggie, remember that we are all gods and what we steadfastly believe and have faith in, is what will eventuate and will work out to our highest advantage.

All our love goes out to you and dear little Jackie.

Maggie has finished her salad, and Palmer puts down the letter.

"I ought to write to my mother one of these days."

Maggie looks at him without saying anything. Not a dubious or scornful look—she is just waiting for him to say whatever else is on his mind.

"Do you need some paper?" she says at last.

"Well, I won't write her just now—it was just a thought. When I get back home—"

"You ought to do it," Maggie says. "But right now it's really time to go get Jackie."

*   *   *

Dear mama. So good of you to write to Maggie. I happen to be down here now too, but pretty soon I'll be starting on the long trek north. Mama, I admire your positive attitude and your indomitable optimism, and when I was younger I too believed that "we are all gods," but since then I have done a lot of thinking, and now it is more like "what fools these mortals be." Maybe sometimes we can feel that everything is beautiful and angels' wings are sprouting from our brains, but that doesn't make us gods. It doesn't, mama.

*   *   *

"Daddy!" Jackie says. He runs across the play area and throws himself into Palmer's arms. One of the nuns is watching with amusement.

"He said his daddy wasn't *ever* going to come," she tells Palmer.

"I'm not *never* coming here again!" Jackie says.

"Why not, doodle?"

"They wouldn't let me swing!"

The nun, still amused, explains to Palmer that it was the younger children's turn on the swings.

"You've got to be patient with the little children, doodle," Palmer says as they go out to the van. "They look up to you. They think you're a giant."

"I thought you were going to go away, daddy."

"I guess I won't be down here too much longer, doodle."

*   *   *

And he has done all that needs to be done. There are no more of these little chores. He has helped Maggie to make a home, but now there is nothing more that needs to be done. This realization hits him when they are buying groceries that evening. He is holding up a fine bunch of tokay grapes, and suddenly he is aware of the dichotomy: everything they buy in this store will have to be either for her or for him. These grapes, for instance—Maggie will never eat these grapes;

these grapes will sustain him on the road. He drops them into the shopping cart.

"*I* wanted to put them in!" Jackie is petulant; Maggie has been letting him be her helper.

"I guess I'll be leaving tomorrow."

"You'll need some sandwiches, then—should we get some more cheese, do you think?"

"You won't be needing me for anything?" Palmer says. "Maybe I should stay and help you look for a car."

"No."

"You'll be needing a car, won't you?"

"I think I can manage without a car . . . You'll be wanting some hard-boiled eggs, won't you?"

"I suppose." Palmer picks up a carton of eggs.

"No, no!" Maggie says. "Let Jackie do it!"

A few minutes later Palmer unthinkingly gets a jug of milk from the case instead of letting Jackie do it, and Jackie begins to sob noisily. It's been a long day for him and he's exhausted.

"Jackie, *you* got some things and *Rob* got some things," Maggie explains. "That's what cooperation is."

"*I* wanted to get the milk!"

"Jackie, I don't want to hear any more crying."

Finally Maggie carries him out to the van in tears, and Palmer waits in line to pay for the groceries. In the wake of Jackie's crying there is a silence like that of a church, except for the sounds of the cash registers. Other parents give Palmer sympathetic smiles, and a little girl squeaks up at her mother:

"What was the little boy crying about, mama?"

"Doan know, sweetheart."

"Is she going to take a switch to him, mama?"

"Ah spect she will, sweetheart. Ah spect she will."

*   *   *

The fishes in Jackie's mobile are swimming slowly back and forth, and lying beneath them Jackie gets his goodnight kiss from Maggie.

"I love you, mama."

"Why Jackie, I love you too."

"But I don't love Rob, because he wouldn't let me get the milk."

"Jackie, that's silly! You should be nice to your dad—he's going to be leaving tomorrow and you won't be seeing him for a while."

Jackie's eyes flit upwards, to the silver fishes, and then to Palmer, and then to Maggie again.

"Rob is going back up to get some more things and then he'll come back here and we'll all be together, and we'll be *sooo* happy!—right, mama?"

Maggie starts to smile, but stops herself. She reaches across Jackie to tuck in the sheet.

"It'll be something like that, Jackie," she says. "But you know Rob isn't coming back right away—he's got work to do up there. Now go to sleep."

"Good-bye, mama."

"Goodnight, Jackie."

"Good-bye, daddy."

"Goodnight, doodle."

*   *   *

Maggie begins to get food together for Palmer's trip. She brings out the peanut butter and the cheese and the bread and puts half a dozen eggs on to boil, and then brings out the old blue vinyl picnic basket her mother gave her and throws in apples, bananas, grapes, and plums.

"How many sandwiches do you want?"

"A lot."

"Four cheese and four peanut butter?"

"I guess." Palmer watches her moving around in the kitchen for a few minutes. "Maggie," he says at last, "maybe we don't have to have a costume party tonight."

She drops the bread on the counter and looks at him.

"Wh-wh-what do you mean?"

"We're not going to be seeing each other for a long time—maybe we could just make love to each *other.*"

"I w-w-wasn't . . . I'm cooking eggs! You mean you want me to get undressed."

"Maggie, Maggie—whatever you want. Forget I said anything!"

"I'll get undressed."

She turns off the eggs and she goes to her bedroom and lies flat on her back like a magnificent naked statue. O dear Maggie, o sweet Maggie, o god, o god Maggie . . . he whispers and he kisses her, he kisses her all over and he whispers little things to her, but she is somewhere else, she is somewhere boiling eggs or somewhere on the great stage, waiting for applause, and at last he closes his eyes and there isn't any Maggie anywhere around, and he is with the girl next door, the blond named Mary Sue . . . she answers the door in a diaphanous nightie and invites him in, and then Miss Naboo is there somehow as well . . . dear Miss Naboo, sweet Miss Naboo, o god Miss Naboooooooooo . . .

*   *   *

Maggie boils the eggs in the morning, standing in the gray kitchen in her panties, and slaps the sandwiches together while Palmer is still dousing his eyes with cold water. When Jackie calls out from his room, they stop what they're doing and look at each other.

"Nnnn-no, Yurii! . . . *I* had it first!"

Just talking in his sleep. Maggie, still holding the butter knife, smiles at Palmer.

"He should be getting up now anyway," she says. "It's late."

They go into his room and stand by his bed a minute, side by side, looking down at him.

"*I*—" Jackie says. "Nnn." His arm falls across his toy bear. For a moment his face is troubled and then it is calm again.

"Jackie! Time to wake up!"

Maggie kneels and touches his shoulder, and Jackie sits up and looks at her.

"Where's my baby?"

"There—right beside you."

"No, my *other* baby!"

"Here he is. His trunk is just a little bent—you must have been lying on him."

"My poor baby!" Jackie croons, clutching his elephant in his arms. "I want to bring my babies to school today, mama."

"Bring whatever you want, Jackie, but hurry—it's time to go."

*   *   *

Palmer lets Maggie out in front of the theater. She gives Jackie a kiss and stretches her hand across to Palmer.

"I'll be seeing you."

"Maybe we can get together sometime," Palmer tells her, holding on to her hand. "Maybe—"

"Well, of course! Of course!"

"Maybe we can get together at Christmas—what do you think?"

"I've got to run—I'm already late. Have a good trip."

She runs up the steps into the theater. Palmer waits a moment, looking at the door that closed behind her, and then drives Jackie to the day-care center.

"I hate to be leaving you, doodle. I won't be seeing you for a long time."

"But we'll be seeing you at Christmas, daddy."

"I'm going to be lonely without you."

One of the nuns is sitting on a wooden bench by the entrance to the play area, smiling at the children, and when Palmer opens the gate to let Jackie in she turns to them and smiles. Palmer squats and holds Jackie in his arms.

"Good-bye, doodle."

"Good-bye, daddy."

Jackie wriggles away. He finds himself a broken plastic truck and sits in the dirt with it. He looks sleepy. Palmer stands outside the gate and watches. The truck doesn't have any wheels. Jackie runs it back and forth absently, and in a few minutes he jerks his head around.

"Daddy!"

"What, doodle?"

"*Go.*"

The nun smiles at Palmer once again, and he smiles at her. And he goes.

*   *   *

Dear mama. There isn't any point in dragging out good-byes but I was never very good at saying good-bye, so that is why my good-bye to Maggie, which should have taken place five minutes after we first met, has taken me ten years. Of course we pretend it is not a real good-bye. Of course we pretend we'll be seeing each other again and this separation is only temporary. I do not think that it is true and I do not think that Maggie thinks that it is true, but mama, I think we have deluded ourselves for ten years, and sometimes I do not know what Maggie thinks is true or what I think is true either. But maybe we *will* see each other again, maybe we will . . .

O mama, it is a long road north, and it is a lonely road. And I wonder: in twenty years or thirty years or forty years from now, will Jackie be traveling on the lonely roads and traveling here and there and back and forth and all across the great wide face of the continent, writing letters in his mind to say the things he cannot say?

You write to me so often and I never write to you. I would like to write and tell you everything, but how can I, mama, how can I?

*   *   *

Palmer stops for coffee at a diner a few miles north of St. Louis. The weather has been changing; in Louisiana it was summer and here it is fall. A cold wind is blowing, and when he opens the back door of the van to look for his wool shirt, Jackie's elephant falls out.

"Damn."

He picks it up from the gravel and dusts it off.

"God *damn* it."

He brings the coffee out to the van in a paper cup and looks at the elephant while he drinks it.

"You goddamned elephant."

It must be Jackie's bedtime already. Palmer sets the elephant on the little red seat beside him and eats one of the cheese sandwiches and a couple of hard-boiled eggs. The coffee is good, and he goes inside for another cup.

"Do you sell postcards?"

"Over there, the rack—see it? That one of the lake is real pretty."

He buys one of the postcards, then borrows the girl's pen while he waits for his coffee to cool.

Dear mama,
   I've taken Jackie down to Maggie and now I'm on my way back home. It's going to be lonely without them but it's going to be all right.

"It looks like a nice lake," he tells the girl.
"We think it's mighty fine."

. . . You can be happy anywhere or you can be unhappy anywhere. Happiness comes from inside you. If you don't find it inside you, you won't find it anywhere.

He drops the card into a mailbox on the way out of town and then follows the signs back to the highway. He has been driving for twelve hours and he's tired. There's a crick in his neck. The coffee didn't do its job; he's going to have to stop for the night.

"What do you think?" he says to the elephant. "You think that everything's going to be all right? You think we're gods? What do you think about that, old buddy? You think that mama is right? You think maybe we're masters of our destiny?"

He gets onto the highway again and follows the red taillights going north. There aren't many people going north.

"Maybe we're not gods and maybe we're not angels, and maybe it doesn't make any real difference how we live our lives—what do you think, old pachyderm? But we have the ability to put meaning into our lives . . . we can give them dignity—we can live with decency and compassion . . . Ole buddy, ah think ah'm *tahrd.*"

*   *   *

At the rest area he parks the van so it is headed south, crawls into the back, pulls the curtains closed, and wraps the sleeping bag around him.

"In the morning we'll drive back down," he whispers to the

elephant. "Back down to Louisiana. That's what we'll do. That's what we'll do. And everything will be all right . . . *Shit*!"

He holds the little elephant against his cheek for a long time. "In the morning, maybe that's what we'll do."

Crater Lake

All the way up the coast Santini had been moody. When Julie, to be pleasant, asked what he was thinking he would say he was thinking about nothing, or about his dissertation. If she asked how the dissertation was coming along, or whether there was a chance that he might get it done before the baby was born, he would grimace for a moment, exhale slowly between his teeth, and explain to her that he was just trying to concentrate on the driving and just hoping that they would be able to find a place to camp that night. But even after they had found their place for the night—after they had set up their tent and finished their dinner and had nothing more to do than sit together on a folded sleeping bag, gazing into the fire and hearing the sweep of wind through pines or the shouts of children beaming their flashlights through the dark—even then (though she knew he was doing his best to talk with her and be open with her) his moodiness did not disperse entirely. It seemed somehow to linger in the background even while he talked (cheerfully, one would have said) about the croissants they had munched in San Francisco, about the raccoons that had made off with their toothpaste a couple of nights before, about the old Austrian couple who had befriended them while hiking in the Canadian Rockies the previous summer, about their two cats back in Los Angeles—did she think Richard would remember to feed them?—and about Richard and some of their other L.A. friends. It came more to the fore, this lingering moodiness, when he mentioned (in passing, and disparagingly) the two sixteen-year-old runaways Richard had brought back to L.A. with him from a hitchhiking trip across the Arizona desert.

That was the reason for all the moodiness, Julie thought, right there: those two runaways (they were running away from their parents, back in Pueblo Bonito, who were cruel and unreasonable). Santini was mad about one of them. He had suddenly taken to spending all his evenings over at Richard's; he had brought the girl to the beach with him and Julie (lending her the orange bikini that Julie could no longer fit into), had invited her to dinner, had even wanted her to accompany them on their trip up the coast. The name of this girl was Lola. She was plump, not particularly pretty, certainly not witty or intelligent, and she wore braces on her teeth.

*   *   *

Their neighbors in the campground at Crater Lake were a couple of blond girls, about twenty, who had arrived late at night and set up their tent to the accompaniment of a radio that blared so loudly that Julie and Santini could not sleep. Santini went into a rage. He unzipped the tent flap, strode out into the cold, moonlit night in his underwear, and shouted for them to shut that goddamn thing off. Surprisingly enough, the girls complied. Julie had fallen asleep almost immediately.

When she awoke in the morning the girls had already driven off, in their little rust-colored beetle, to explore the terrain, and Santini was already up. Julie found him sitting at the picnic table, eating cold cereal and writing on a yellow legal pad.

"Writing letters?"

"Yes."

"Who to?"

"A friend," Santini said. "I mean, my mother." He laughed and shook his head. "I don't mean my mother—I mean Richard! I'm writing Richard now—I'm going to write my mother next. I'm just *finishing* this letter to Richard, and that's why I said my mother. I'm just about to write to her."

"I don't care who you're writing to," Julie said, wounded by so much dishonesty so early in the morning. She had no doubt in the world that he had been writing to Lola, his chubby little runaway. While Santini finished his letter and stuck it into an envelope, Julie pumped the gasoline stove, lit one of its burners, and put water on for coffee.

"Do you know Richard's address?" Santini said.

"It's still three-nineteen Canoga."

"I just wanted to make sure he remembered to feed the cats."

That he should feel the need to write to Lola did not hurt her so much as that he should feel the need to lie to her about it. But whoever he had been writing to, the letter seemed to have put him in a better frame of mind. While she was still waiting for the water to boil he came up behind her and put his arms around her; he clasped his hands gently on her belly and nibbled the back of her neck.

"How's the mommy?" he said. "Did you sleep okay, my honeybunny? Did the porcupine wake you?"

Julie put her hands on his and closed her eyes for a moment before answering. She had slept okay. She had woken once or twice, but not because of any porcupine. Had there really been a porcupine?

*   *   *

Santini had a variety of paperbound nature guides, and the one she had given him for his birthday, *Wildflowers of the Cascades,* he brought along when they left the car at the Sun Notch parking lot to hike up toward the caldera rim. In another of his guides, the one on North American mammals, he had shown her a picture of a porcupine like the one he had seen the night before—it had been nosing into the tin cans someone had left in the fireplace, and when it finally sauntered away it was carrying an empty plastic bread wrapper in its mouth—and as they hiked he kept looking for trees with bark eaten away around the base, which, he said, would be evidence of porcupines.

But there weren't many trees of any sort; it was fields they were walking through, full of high grass and wildflowers. Santini would stop by some of the flowers and look them up in his book; sometimes he would take a leaf or two to press between the pages. With him, besides the wildflower book, he had brought the information sheet on Crater Lake, and he read aloud from it as he trudged beside her up the hill.

"Bears and deer," he said. "Eagles and hawks, sometimes foxes, coyotes, *por*cupines, it says here, and what else? Various birds, chipmunks, ground squirrels. Golden-mantled ground squirrels."

"Does it really say bears?"

"They're especially fond of eating pregnant ladies, it says here."

"Are there really bears?"

"That's what it says. And listen to this: *Remember, animals may bite—and even a small nip can be serious.* Like General Tojo— he was serious, wasn't he?"

It had been cold in the morning when she left the tent, but now the sun and the climbing were making Julie hot. Sweat ran down her face and her back and her breasts. Santini took off his sweater and then his shirt.

"I don't think there'd be any bears up in this area," he said. "It's a large park. They'd probably stay away from people."

"Do you suppose it's very much further?"

"You're tired," Santini said. "We don't have to continue, my honeybunny. We can sit down for a while if you want."

"I'm not tired, I'm just hot. Shouldn't we be following some sort of trail?"

"I didn't see any trail. If you're hot, take your dress off."

"O, fine idea."

"Nobody's going to see. Let's just sit down for a while." Santini kicked off his sneakers and unbuckled his belt. He began pulling his jeans off.

"Nate, somebody's going to come by!"

"Nobody's going to come by—we haven't seen anybody for half an hour. Would you rather go over there?" He pointed toward a grove of shrubs and four or five aspens in a small ravine fifty yards away.

Julie did not answer. She looked around to see if there was anybody watching them, but he was right: there was no one. From the road where they had left their car she heard occasional sounds of traffic, and from the field around them the whisper of grasses, the scintillant thrum of insects. The insect sounds, the clear blue sky, the sunshine: how could she argue with all nature? In a few minutes she took her own clothes off and joined Santini in the grass.

The sweet smell of the grass, the warm sun, the drone of a distant airplane: these things, as they lay together on their spread-out clothes, produced a pleasant drowsiness in her; she felt she could lie there naked under the sun, in her hus-

band's arms, for hours. The plane she had heard flew closer
and passed overhead, not very high at all—an airliner, it
looked like. As the sound of the plane faded off to the west, she
raised her head in alarm.

"O god," she said, "do you hear somebody? Is that somebody singing?"

"No." Santini did not open his eyes.

Julie got to her knees and peered over the top of the tall
grass. She could see no one, but she heard voices and laughter.

"God, it is. Somebody's coming this way."

"Christ." Santini sprang to his feet, grabbed up their
clothes, and started running for the trees in the ravine. Halfway there he remembered Julie, and turned back to help her.
She was jogging awkwardly, trying to support her belly with
one hand and with the other her breasts, which with pregnancy had become so large, for the first time in her life, as to be
unmanageable. Santini stared at these big breasts as if he had
only now become aware of their existence.

"Go ahead," she said. "What are you doing?"

"I was going to help you."

"I don't need any help."

They made it to the little grove in the ravine before anyone
came into sight, and Julie knelt behind the bushes to look
through the armful of clothes Santini had thrown down. Santini looked on unhappily while her breasts disappeared into a
brassiere.

"There's no need to get dressed."

"God, Nate, if there are people out there I want my clothes
on!"

"They're not going to come over *here*—we're perfectly safe."

"What happened to my panties?"

"Why don't we just lie down again for a while, okay, my
honeybunny?"

Julie was still picking through the clothes. "Did you get my
panties? I don't see my panties."

"Did you wear any?"

"Nate, of *course* I wear panties! Do you think I'm one of
Richard's little friends?"

"You want me to run out there and see if I can find them?"

"Don't be idiotic." He was still naked except for his feet, which he had jammed partway into his torn yellow sneakers. "For god's sake, just get down."

"Here they come!" Santini whispered.

He dropped to her side and grabbed for his jeans, which he tried to pull on over his sneakers. They became stuck at the level of his knees, and while he was still struggling to get them higher Julie began to see some of the people whose voices she had heard. She could only see the tops of their heads at first. They were coming up the hill the way she and Santini had come, eight or ten teenagers, both boys and girls, perhaps following the path she and Santini had inadvertently blazed through the field. As they came closer she could see that three of the boys were wearing dark green scouting shirts. A couple of the boys were shirtless, and one of these, the last in line, carried a canteen—its strap a dark slash across his pale chest—and a long black branch that he used as a walking stick. One of the boys with shirts on started singing, "We're on the upward trail," and then broke off with a laugh.

"Christ," Santini whispered.

"Sh."

The scouts had come to where she and Santini had been lying earlier. The boy in the lead stopped, reached down into the grass, and brought up between thumb and forefinger a pair of pink panties, which he tossed into the air. One of the shirtless boys caught them and pulled them down over his ears for a moment like a mobcap. He turned, twirling them on a fingertip, to offer them to the petite, cute redhead behind him, who held them in front of her hips, giggled with delight, and did a brief hula before passing them on. The next girl in line tossed them down into the grass, but they were rescued again by the boy with the canteen. He jabbed the end of his stick into them and held it up so they fluttered in the breeze like the pennon of a conquering army.

Julie watched this pink flag following the hikers up the hill. She looked at Santini, who had finally gotten his pants on.

"Well, now we can get undressed again," he said.

"I'm not getting undressed again."

"You sure?"

"I'm not getting undressed again!"

"I was just joking," Santini said. "Christ, what a sense of humor." He grabbed his shirt and his sweater and his wild-flower book and started out into the field. "Are you coming?"

"Where are you going?"

"To see the lake, I suppose."

"I'm going back to the car."

"To the car? What for? Don't you want to see the lake?"

"We can see it someplace else, can't we?"

"We're almost there! It can't be much further."

"I'm going back to the car."

"May I ask why?" Santini said.

"Why do you think?"

"You're afraid that if we see those kids they'll know they're your panties? Is that what you think?"

"I don't know what they'll think. I don't want to think about it. I don't want to see them again. I want to go back to the car."

"Christ," said Santini. "Okay. Let's not see the lake. Let's go back to the damned car."

*   *   *

They saw the scouts again, late in the afternoon, halfway down the Cleetwood trail—which (according to the blue information sheet) was the only safe route down to the water. This trail, held in place by logs embedded in the dry earth, descended by means of sharp switchbacks; and several switchbacks below them Julie could see the scouts—five of them at least—coming up as she and Santini went down. She should have known they would be here; at the head of the trail she had seen the same yellow schoolbus, presumably theirs, that she had noticed earlier at the Sun Notch parking lot.

"Let's go back up," she said to Santini.

"What? What for?"

"They're coming up—those kids. They're down there."

"So what?"

Santini smoothed his hand up and down her back. He looked puzzled and concerned. In a moment Julie laughed.

"I must sound really nutty. I don't know what I was thinking. I keep thinking they saw us. Or that they'd know those were my panties."

"It's okay, my honeybunny. My little nutty buddy."

"They wouldn't have any way of knowing, would they?"

"We can ask them."

Below them the lake was like a second sky, its surface unruffled by wind, placid, perfectly mirroring, blue. A tour boat, filled with sightseers, shivered this blue mirror as it headed for shore. Over the sound of the tour boat's engines Julie could hear a woman's tinny, amplified voice warning the passengers to remain seated until the boat was docked.

In a few minutes the boat tied up at its pier, and by the time Julie and Santini reached the foot of the trail the passengers, a motley crowd of young and old—many of them sunburned and most looking pleasantly tired—were starting the long climb to the top. She and Santini stood aside to let them pass. Other sightseers were already climbing aboard the boat for the next tour.

It would have been nice to join them—to go out on the peaceful, quintessentially azure water for a while and gaze at the ancient volcano's walls that rose above the lake like a giant teacup's rim—but she and Santini did not have the money; and even if they'd had the money the restfulness of the boat ride would have been ruined anyway by the tinny, monotonous spiel of the tour guide. Santini was already heading out onto the smaller pier, where rowboats were for hire and where four more of the kids they had seen earlier were looking out at the lake.

Three of them were sitting on the edge of the pier with their feet dangling in the water: the boy with the canteen, the little redhead, and another girl whose black, tightly curled hair shone in the sunlight as though oiled. The fourth, a tall boy in a forest-green shirt emblazoned with award patches, stood beside them, and his legs, naked between the bottoms of his shorts and the tops of his hiking boots, were so long and thin that to Julie they looked like the legs of a crane.

Santini went over to this boy and began talking about scouting. He had been a scout himself but he had never made it to eagle. He had always regretted that. He had become a life scout but had gone no further. The boy answered in polite mono-syllables. Julie, meanwhile, noticed that the boy with the can-teen not only still had his stick—he was holding it out over the water like a fishing pole—but still had her panties on the end of it. He dunked them in and out of the water like fish bait. Julie went over to the opposite side of the pier and watched the sightseers being herded into their seats in the tour boat. She was embarrassed not so much by the public display of her underwear as by Santini's attempt at making friends with the kids, which seemed to her, as she was sure it must seem to the kids, gratuitous and fumbling.

"When I was a scout," Santini said, "we never used to have girls in the scouts."

"No sir," the tall boy said. "That happens sometimes now, but actually these are girl scouts."

"Hi, girl scouts," Santini said.

"*Hi*, girl scouts," the boy with the canteen mimicked softly. The two girls looked at each other and then smiled at Santini and said hello. The redhead turned to look at Julie, who was pretending still to be caught up in the departure of the tour boat from the other pier, and then whispered something to the black-haired girl. The black-haired girl laughed.

"Actually," the tall boy said, "these women are such bitches we wouldn't *want* them in our troop."

"They don't look that terrible to me," Santini said. He leaned over and spoke to the redhead. "Are you really that bad? Are you as terrible as he says?"

"I don't know."

"How's the water? Cold?"

"I guess."

The boy with the canteen whispered something to the red-head, and she laughed and punched his arm. Santini pulled off his shoes and socks and sat down next to the redhead to stick his feet into the water.

"Ooo. Cold."

"Too cold for me," the redhead said, smiling at him. She removed her feet from the water and stood up.

In a few minutes the scouts left. Santini remained on the edge of the pier, looking out onto the lake with a fixed smile on his face. Julie went over and sat down near him and dipped her own toes into the cold water, but did not look at him or otherwise intrude upon his silence.

At length Santini turned and gave her one of the innocent-little-boy smiles that had first endeared him to her and endeared him to her even now. Despite his week's growth of beard, he looked like a five-year-old in need of cosseting.

"I was going to try to rescue your panties," he said, "but obviously my sly maneuvering didn't achieve the desired results."

An astounding lie. Santini kept smiling at her, and Julie, shaking her head, said, "God, you must think I'm really stupid."

Santini took this as a cue to move over and put his arm around her. "My little honeybunny, I don't think that at all. You're the smartest little mommy on the whole pier."

*   *   *

On the way back to the campground Santini kept saying things like, "I'm glad we were able to come. It's really nice to be here with you. This may be the last camping we do alone for a long time." He reached over and patted her stomach. All of this, she knew, was in response to her quietness, which made him uneasy. When they got back to the campground he insisted on cooking dinner for his little mommy. And while the foil-wrapped potatoes blackened in the coals he spoke about his dissertation—on guilds in medieval Florence—more enthusiastically than he had, it seemed to her, in over a year. "Maybe I *will* get it done before the baby's born. What I really hope is I can get somebody to publish it—some little academic press, maybe."

"Do you think it's possible?"

"It's *possible.*"

"Nate, do you think the potatoes are done?"

"You really give a shit about my dissertation."

Santini turned angrily and squatted by the fire. He jabbed a fork into one of the potatoes and thumped it onto the table. The other potato he rolled out of the coals with a stick.

"I do care about your dissertation. If you could get it published, that'd be great. But what am I supposed to say about it? You never tell me anything about it, you never want to talk about it."

Santini ignored what she had said and occupied himself with unwrapping the potatoes. "They look as though they're about done. I hope the hamburgers haven't gotten too cold."

"If you don't want to talk about the dissertation, why do you bring it up?"

"There's nothing to say about it."

"Maybe there's nothing to say about anything."

"There's nothing to say about the dissertation."

Julie went to the car and got the half-gallon of burgundy that had been baking in the trunk all day. She poured some into two plastic cups and drank a little from hers before sitting down across from Santini at the picnic table. The wine was very warm. Santini smiled at her.

"Are you pissed?"

"Why should I be? If you don't want to talk about your dissertation we don't have to. We can talk about your girlfriends instead."

"I don't have any," Santini said. "Only one. Or rather, two. You and—" He pointed to her belly.

"Me and little Lola."

"That would be a *terrible* name for a baby."

"Me and little Potatohead. Me and little Pootiepie. Me and little Scootface."

"Stop it," Santini said. He set down the fork with which he had begun to attack his potato and frowned at her. "Why do you do that? Why do you make up stupid names for it? Do you think that's good? What's the point of being negative about it?"

This sudden seriousness of his amazed Julie; it seemed to her hypocritical and unjust.

"Am *I* being negative?"

"What's the point of it?"

"Why is it always *me* who's being negative? You think you've got such a great sense of humor. Why is it always *me* who's saying stupid things?"

"Honey. Honey."

"Is everything you say bright and positive? *I'm* not negative. This baby is a part of me. I'm going to love this baby."

Santini got up and came around the table and stood behind
her with his hands on her shoulders. He rubbed the back of her
neck gently with his thumbs to placate her. "Honey, I know
you are."

"I think you're a real bastard."

"I *am,*" he admitted happily.

"You think you can make everything a joke and that makes
it okay."

"I thought you knew I was a bastard. I thought that's why
you married me."

She shrugged her shoulders to get his hands off her. "Okay,
you're very funny. Why don't you sit down? Let's eat."

"Your muscles are tight. You're tense."

"I'm tense with hunger. Let's eat."

*　　　*　　　*

For an hour or two afterward, while she and Santini sat by
the dying fire, Julie was feeling unreasonably happy. Perhaps
their brief quarrel had been a sort of catharsis—she didn't
often get the opportunity to call Santini a bastard—but the
happiness seemed more a physical than a mental thing: it
came from the wine, from her tiredness from hiking and being
in the sun, and from the crisp night air punctuated with camp-
ers' voices and the occasional hooting of an owl. Somewhere in
another part of the campground a radio was playing, but not
objectionably: it was harpsichord music, Vivaldi perhaps, and
so far away and soft that it might have been the music of the
spheres. The girls at the next campsite brought out their own
enormous noisebox as soon as they returned to camp and set it
on the picnic table next to the blazing propane lantern, but
refrained, for the moment, from turning it on. One of the
girls—the short-haired one, the more attractive of the two—
stood by the table and tapped her foot on the bench to unheard
music while she gobbled cold beef stew from a can. The other,
Julie saw, was pouring motor oil onto the logs piled in the fireplace.

"I guess I shouldn't have yelled at them," Santini said. "Maybe I should apologize."

"Wait and see if they keep their radio off."

The girls were joined by a couple of boys whom Julie had noticed earlier, on her way back from the latrine, when they had squealed into the campground in a mud-splattered yellow jeep. The one who had been driving, who was red-bearded and fair of hair, laughed and made sounds of choking when the girls lit their fire. The oil on the logs burned with an orange flame and gave off a thick black smoke that rose sluggishly above the treetops and obscured the stars.

Julie, mildly annoyed by the smell of the burning oil, looked at Santini and waited for him to make some comment (the little Santini in her mind had already made sardonic reference to the pristine purity of the mountain air), but he, perhaps still absorbed by the question of whether or not to apologize, seemed oblivious to this further assault on his senses, and he said nothing. He did not speak for some time. He poked at the fire with a stick, sipped some wine, and occupied himself with his own thoughts, which might (Julie supposed) as easily be of Florentine guilds as of rolling naked through fields of daisies with nubile Lola.

Julie was feeling drowsy. She was on the verge of retiring to the tent for the night when Santini suddenly got to his feet and said, "Let's go make friends."

"Nate, do you think—?"

"Come on."

He was already on his way, holding the bottle of burgundy out in front of him as he lurched through the underbrush that separated the two campsites, and Julie, against her best judgment, followed. Away from the campfire, the night was cold. One of the blond girls, she saw, the rather chunky one, had wrapped herself up in a sleeping bag to keep warm, and the other was being warmed by the bearded boy—her head on his shoulder, her eyes closed, her body enfolded by his arm and the wing of his coat. When Santini burst into their campsite the girl in the sleeping bag looked up but the other girl did not even open her eyes. The bearded boy stared at Santini without understanding, as though he believed him to be an apparition.

The other boy, who wore a green sweatshirt that said "Save Coon River," did not look up from what he was doing, which was using a broken plastic fork to inscribe geometric figures in the dirt near the picnic table. Santini held the wine bottle by the neck and shook it.

"Like some wine?"

The girl in the sleeping bag glanced at her friend, whose eyes remained closed, then shrugged and said, "Why not?"

After half a minute the bearded boy, still staring at Santini, let go of the breath he had been holding—Julie was suddenly aware that they were smoking dope, that they had probably been smoking it for hours even before returning to the campground, and that they were all stoned out of their skulls—and exploded into a whoop of laughter. "Wine! Great. Bee-*yoo*-tiful!" At this, the short-haired girl opened her eyes, smiled, and accepted the joint he handed her. She took a brief hit and held it out to Santini, who in return handed her the bottle.

Despite the wine she had drunk, Julie was uncomfortable among these stoned, uninteresting strangers, and it amazed her both that Santini should have wanted to make friends with them and that he should believe, as he seemed to, that he had succeeded. She watched him lifting the joint to his lips and going through his slow ritual. He inhaled deeply, exaggeratedly, with his eyes closed, and then, smiling as though the marijuana had satisfied a great need, he squatted beside the girl in the sleeping bag to offer the joint to her. She passed it on immediately, but Santini remained at her side, grinning, now, with the painful obsequiousness of desire.

So that was what it was all about? Santini had looked over and seen that one of these girls was unencumbered, and had decided to move in? Julie sat down by herself at the picnic table and, occasionally sipping from the cup of wine she had carried with her, she thought, without rancor, about Santini's motivations. He was talking, now, in low tones, to the girl in the sleeping bag, but she clearly had no interest in him whatsoever. Didn't he realize that? Julie ran her fingers over the girls' large, chromey, silent radio and rotated the station knob. The girl in the sleeping bag and the boy in the green sweatshirt—those two had certainly been left out in the cold. All those two wanted to do, Julie imagined, was to get on with their separate camping trips; but fate or the god of young lovers or of dopers had brought the four of them together, the boys in their yellow jeep, the girls in their wheezing beetle, at some flower-choked trailhead or scenic overlook along the rim drive, and an explosion of lust or love had blasted their plans to fragments and regrouped the two-plus-two into a one-plus-two-plus-one of uncertain half-life: the lucky couple still burbling in the first ecstasy of discovering each other in the wilds of Oregon, and the other disgruntled, extraneous two, these two separate mopers, one in a sleeping bag and one in a sweatshirt demanding the salvation of Coon River, who wanted nothing to do with each other, who wanted only to get this nonsense over with and get back to whatever it was (the call of nature? of adventure? of friendship?) for whose sake they had headed north in the first place to Crater Lake.

The boy with the green sweatshirt had gotten to his feet to offer her a joint—this was several joints later—and when Julie declined he passed it on and then sat down beside her. He was thin and taller than Santini, with straight chestnut hair that kept falling onto his forehead (he brushed it back with his fingertips) and a jaw that seemed too large for his face.

"What I've been meaning to ask you—" he said. "Well, this is going to sound stupid, but—"

He smiled and shook his head at his own inarticulateness. He looked down at his hands, which he had spread flat on the tabletop with the fingers splayed wide as for the attentions of an invisible manicurist.

"What?"

"I hope this isn't offensive, but: Are you pregnant, or are you just fat?"

"Just fat," Julie said.

"Well, you're a really pretty fat lady."

This, because of its unexpectedness and the shy manner of its delivery, seemed to Julie the loveliest compliment she had ever received. (A few minutes later, when he found that she lived in Hollywood, he tried to give her another—he said she must be a movie star incognito—but that one was so trite that the kindest thing to do was pretend he had not said it.) His

name was Clark, he was originally from Florida, he was study-
ing microbiology at San Francisco State, and so on . . . but all
that vaporous wordstuff vanished into the night as readily as
the smoke from the campfire. What was important was his
physical presence, the sound of his voice, his interest in her.
She liked talking to him. She allowed the conversation to
become flirtatious, and when, after twenty minutes or so, she
stood up and said she really thought it was time for her to be
getting to bed, she was not surprised that he asked if she
would like him to come with her.

Yes, she would. She longed to be held, if only for a moment,
in the arms of a stranger. But she did not say that. She ignored
his question and told him only that she had enjoyed talking to
him.

*   *   *

She was drifting off to sleep when Santini came into the
tent, but she sat up and, as he crawled into his sleeping bag,
asked him if he wanted a divorce. This question felt as though
it had been on her mind all evening, and if she did not ask it
now she knew she would not have the courage to ask it in the
morning.

Santini sat up and looked at her. "Christ," he said. "Jesus,
Julie."

"Is that what you want? I know it's late, but you should be
able to tell me that, shouldn't you? You must know whether
you want a divorce?"

Santini's lip began to quiver and in a minute he turned away,
sniffling, to rub his eyes with the back of his hand.

"Don't you love me? Aren't you my honey?"

"Nate, I don't know what you *want*. What do you *want*? You
want somebody who isn't pregnant? You want somebody
who's sixteen or eighteen—is that what you want? Somebody
like Lola?"

"But she won't have me!" he cried. "She doesn't love me!"

And he began to tell Julie, who sat stunned by his passion-
ate recitation of things she had suspected all along, about the
misery he was going through for Lola's sake. How she

wouldn't go to bed with him. How she wouldn't take him seriously. How she believed there was no hope for them because he was already married.

"Well," Julie said when he stopped talking, "the course of true love is a rocky one, I guess."

"O my honey," he cried, awkwardly embracing her sleeping bag, "O my honey, my honey! Why am I such a louse? Why do I have to hurt you this way?"

He rested his head against her bosom and as, reflexively, she began to stroke his hair, he attempted to explain himself, to discover reasons for his wandering eye. It was because of the great coldness of his upbringing, he concluded, that he was unfaithful—that terrible coldness when he was just a child. It was because he had never been loved.

"Sh," she said. "Sh. It's all right. *I* love you."

And, still caressing his hair and his unshaven cheeks, she felt vaguely that some conclusion had been reached, and that some good must come out of all this; but just what it would be, she did not know.

Rainfall

The rain started pattering against the old Dodge almost before they had left the outskirts of Des Moines, and to Peter Blackburn, the driver, it did not look as though it would stop before they got to Boston. It was gray and chilly out. Blackburn, nursing a wad of sourish fruit-flavored gum as he drove, stared intently past the clicking windshield wipers and gripped the steering wheel as though he feared it might fly away. Behind him, slouched comfortably across the back seat, was his eleven-year-old, Dilly, who divided his energies between nibbling his way through the ginger cookies his mother had packed and fiddling tiredly (he had been up too late the night before) with Blackburn's light meter.

"Are you ever going to see her again?" Dilly said, twirling the light meter's dial.

"Sure," Blackburn said. "What's the matter with you? Of *course* we'll still see each other. We're still your parents, after all."

"Duh."

"It's only a separation," Blackburn said.

But that was not all it was, and he already missed her, grievously. The passenger seat beside him, where she had sat chattering brightly on so many past trips, seemed now to contain an emptiness so vast it could swallow him up forever.

The boy pointed the light meter at the back of Blackburn's head and pretended to take a picture with it. "How soon are we going to stop?"

"We've got a long trip ahead of us. Don't start bugging me about stopping."

Dilly ate another ginger cookie and pointed the light meter out at the gray countryside. The rain was coming down in sheets.

*   *   *

Right before the Indiana border Blackburn had to slow for a

traffic jam. It was a few hours after dark. Dilly, who had fallen asleep in the back seat, woke up when Blackburn touched the brakes to avoid plowing into a semi.

"Lookit the cows," Dilly said groggily.

The cattle were in the semi ahead. Their matted flanks and damp stoic faces were visible through its slats. The semi moved forward a foot or two and then stopped again. Dilly leaned forward, smelling of ginger cookies, and rested his chin on the seatback an inch from Blackburn's shoulder.

"We'll have to get some dinner, Dilly-o. You're probably starving."

"I'm not."

"You'd probably like a nice rare steak. Moooo!"

The boy did not respond. He looked dazed and disoriented from his sleep.

"We'll stop at the next exit," Blackburn said. "I could eat a substantial portion of a cow myself."

The traffic eased forward a foot at a time, and the windshield wipers of the old Dodge kept pace with a hesitant *click-click-click* and a slap of loose rubber that sounded like fingers snapping.

Dilly leaned further forward and pointed at the odometer.

"Dad! Look at that!"

It was only five or six miles short of the hundred thousand mark. While Blackburn waited for the semi to move, Dilly kept his elbows on the seatback and watched the odometer. In forty-five minutes they moved forward only three tenths of a mile.

*   *   *

Then suddenly the semi pulled away and Blackburn could see at last what had caused all the slowing of traffic: in front of them, in the low area beneath an overpass, there was a lake of rainwater that covered all the eastbound lanes of the freeway (the westbound lanes, separated from the eastbound by an impermeable concrete barrier, were fine) and stretched ahead of them for a quarter of a mile.

"O Jesus Christ," Blackburn said.

The semi was pushing its way through the water easily

enough, but how could a car get through? Some cars must have made it, but several obviously had not; they had been abandoned, in water almost up to their windows, beneath the overpass. They bobbed in the wake of the semi like corks. Wavelets lapped the pavement in front of the Dodge.

"Shouldn't we try it, dad? Other cars are making it."

Blackburn stared helplessly after the semi's receding lights. The water looked awfully deep, but it was true that cars in the next lane of traffic were trying it and evidently getting through without too much difficulty. And what alternative was there? There was no way to turn around, no place to turn off. People behind, not yet seeing what the problem was, were honking their horns impatiently. Blackburn glanced into the rearview mirror. Traffic was backed up for miles.

"Everybody seems to be making it okay," Dilly said.

"Stop talking, Dill—just let me think."

Mistrustfully, knowing he was doing the wrong thing, Blackburn went ahead and plunged the old Dodge forward into the water. He tried to follow the route the semi had taken. The water got deeper and deeper. Halfway in, the engine stopped dead.

"O god damn it," Blackburn said. The car was surrounded by water; it was seeping through the doors and rushing up through the floorboards. The headlights and wipers were still on, but he could not get the engine restarted. When he turned the key there was a little clicking sound, like the sound of an angered beetle, and then nothing.

Another semi was passing them now, dangerously close— only inches, it seemed, to their right—and the Dodge too, like the cars that had been abandoned, was set to bobbing in its wake. Blackburn switched off the lights and the wipers, and for a moment buried his face in his hands in an attitude of such weakness and anxiety that Dilly, alarmed, leaned forward and hugged him around the neck.

"Dad!"

"Okay," Blackburn said. "I'm okay." He pushed his door open, jumped out into cold water that came to his thighs and, thrusting himself against the door frame, began to push the car forward, up the slight incline toward dry land. Dilly clambered over the seatback and tried to help by steering. In a couple of minutes Blackburn had the car up to where the water was just over his shoes. He got in and set the handbrake. His hands were shaking from the effort of moving the car. He wiped them on his pants and tried the ignition again, but still without results.

"Maybe we're out of gas," Dilly said.

Blackburn did not answer. He stared at the little red light on the dashboard as though he believed it might show him the way out of this mess. He turned the ignition key again and listened to the clicking. Ahead of him, on the side of the road, there were five or six other cars that must also have stalled in the water. A couple of the drivers were out looking at their engines. They got their cars started and drove away.

"I don't know what it is," Blackburn said after a while. "Probably the battery, now. I shouldn't have kept trying the engine. It probably drained the battery. We'll have to try to get a jump from somebody."

"Maybe we should call a gas station."

"Dilly, just let me think about this, okay?"

He got out again and gazed back toward the water under the overpass. Other cars were still trying to get through, and every so often they stalled as the Dodge had done. As he watched, a small blue car came to a stop in the water; its headlights flickered and went out, and in a minute its driver, a young red-bearded man in a trenchcoat, got out into the water and began to push.

Blackburn, already soaked, waded in and lent his shoulder on the other side. Inside the car, steering, was a blond woman in a nurse's uniform. When they had gotten the car up into the shallows behind Blackburn's Dodge, the young man thanked Blackburn. He went to the front of his car and opened the hood.

"Listen," Blackburn said, "I think I need a jump. My battery must be low. I can't seem to get my car started."

"Seems to be a contagious problem," the young man said, bending over his engine. His girlfriend, meanwhile, had begun taking items of food and clothing out of the car, examining them to see what had gotten soaked or ruined. She set a plastic vanity case and a dripping red sleeping bag on top of the car and then tossed a soggy box of crackers over to the side of the road.

"I've got cables," Blackburn said. "I've got them in my trunk."

The young man loosened a couple of clips on his distributor cap and straightened up again.

"I can't give you any help there. You've got a twelve-volt battery—mine is just a six. A jump probably isn't what you need anyway. Your points are probably wet. You check your points?"

"The points?" Blackburn had only the vaguest idea about what went on inside an engine; he was not sure whether the points were the same as the spark plugs or whether they were something else—were they perhaps something in the distributor?

"Chances are if you get your points dry, it'll start right up."

"So I just—?"

"I'll give you a hand in a minute. But a hundred to one that's what it is. Why don't you go ahead and take the cap off?"

"Distributor cap?"

"I'll give you a hand in a minute."

Thankful to have something to do, Blackburn went back to the Dodge. Dilly was standing some distance away, in water up to his knees, watching the slow oncoming traffic: the semis making their way around the cars abandoned beneath the overpass.

"Get back from the trucks!" Blackburn yelled.

The boy turned and plodded toward him. Blackburn opened the hood of the Dodge and looked in at the engine.

"Did you call me, dad?"

"Why were you standing in the water? Why get your damn feet wet?"

"They're already wet. Is that guy going to help us?"

"He wants to get his own car started first. Dilly, I don't like to see you getting so close to the traffic."

The boy stood beside him, looking into the engine. "This thing," Blackburn said, pointing, "is called the distributor. I don't know much about it, but he seemed to think it might have gotten wet inside."

"Would that keep us from going?"

"He seemed to think so."

Dilly watched while he unplugged the cap and took it off. The young man, Blackburn saw, had been right; there was water in the distributor cap. While he looked in the car for something to dry it off with, he heard behind him the engine of the blue car give a few coughs and then catch.

*   *   *

The girl was at the wheel. She drove up and parked, with the engine still running, in front of the Dodge. The young man, wiping his hands on a pink cloth, walked over. He looked at the distributor cap Blackburn held out to him.

"You took the cables off?"

"I shouldn't have done that?"

Instead of answering, the young man bent over the engine. He wiped his pink cloth carefully around inside the distributor for a few minutes and then straightened up and looked at Blackburn.

"You remember which cables went where?"

"Not exactly."

The young man gave a tired, ironic smile. He glanced toward his own car, where Blackburn could hear the woman changing the radio from station to station.

"You don't take the cables off. You just lift the distributor cap with the cables intact. It's dried off pretty good now, but it's not going to do much good if you don't know which cables go where."

"You don't think it'll start?"

"What, if the cables are connected wrong? If you've got the cylinders firing out of order? Is that going to turn the engine over? That's not going to do anything. It'll be each cylinder for itself."

Blackburn stood there looking at the engine, praying the young man would be able to tell him what could be done. For a minute neither of them spoke.

"Don't know what else I can do," the young man said. "We've got to be going. Give you a ride to the next town?"

Blackburn refused automatically, but he knew, as the little

blue car drove away, that he should not have. There was a great weariness in him. He put his hand on Dilly's shoulder.

"Will we be able to get started, dad?"

"I don't know," Blackburn said. "Why don't you get into the car, Dilly? You want to stay warm."

"I'm okay," Dilly said. "Are you okay? *You* can get into the car if you want to, dad."

*   *   *

It was getting colder out now; a wind had started up, and it cut against his wet clothing and made him shiver violently.

"Maybe we'll have to get a tow. I should have let those people give us a ride."

"Maybe we should hitchhike."

"Maybe we'll have to."

"Want me to try to flag somebody down?"

"No, old Dilly. That's okay. Maybe I can get the car started. I'll look at it again. I'll give it another try."

While Blackburn bent over the engine to try to rearrange the distributor connections Dilly watched the oncoming traffic—the semis and occasional cars threading their way past the abandoned vehicles that still sat in the water beneath the overpass. Six or seven cars had been abandoned there now, and the only way the semis could get by was to go far over on the shoulder.

"This was really stupid," Blackburn said.

"It wasn't *your* fault."

"I should never have driven into that water. That was a really stupid thing to do."

"That was awful," Dilly said.

The boy seemed to assume that the worst was behind them. Blackburn reached over to rub the back of his neck. He got into the car and tried the ignition again.

When he looked out the window he saw Dilly standing in the shallow water with his thumb stuck out like a hitchhiker. Dilly waded in deeper.

"Don't get yourself all wet," Blackburn called. "What the hell is the point of that?"

"I'm wet already, so what's the difference?"

"Dilly, please don't get so close to the traffic! These semis can't see you out here."

"Maybe we can get a ride with somebody."

"Stay back from the traffic!" Blackburn said.

He did not know whether Dilly had heard him or not, and he wondered wearily whether he should go after him and bring him back to the car. Dilly was getting into water up to his thighs, and the semis seemed hardly even to slow down; they thrust waves against him as they roared past.

"Dilly, be careful," Blackburn said.

But the boy was getting old enough, he knew, to take care of himself. For him, Blackburn thought, perhaps it was all an adventure; it would be something to tell his friends about. And anyway he was too tired to keep telling Dilly what to do. He himself did not know, in his exhaustion, what to do, and perhaps the boy was right: perhaps somebody would stop, seeing this pathetic little figure standing out there in the middle of the black water with his thumb stuck out forlornly, and would give them a ride to the nearest town. They would be able to sit in a warm restaurant and drink hot chocolate.

"Poor kid," Blackburn whispered.

He looked at Dilly once more, and then bent tiredly over the engine. He took off the distributor cap again and looked beneath it. He looked at the little copper flange inside the distributor and he looked at the wires that were supposed to lead from the cap to the spark plugs, and he tried to make sense of it all. What order were the wires supposed to be in? What order had they been in before he had pulled them off? He tried desperately to remember that, but at the time their order had not seemed important to him, and remembering it now was an impossibility. What order *would* the wires go in? he asked himself. In what order would the cylinders fire? But he could not reason it out. All he could do, it seemed to him, was to attach the wires at random and hope for the best.

He tried six or seven different permutations of the wires. None seemed to work. But even if the wires *were* in the right order, he knew, the battery was surely drained by now. He sat in the driver's seat holding onto the steering wheel and looking at the little red light on the dashboard, then turned the key again so the light went out. It was such an exhausting business; such a damned exhausting business. If only someone could stop to help!

Suddenly Blackburn felt a twinge of alarm; it was like a sudden jolt of electricity through his brain. What was it—had Dilly called his name?

He twisted around in the seat, but could not see the boy. Blackburn stepped out of the car and looked out over the dark water beneath the overpass. Diesel fumes hung in the air. The waves from a semi that had just passed by were splashing against the concrete barrier. Where was the boy?

"Dilly!" Blackburn shouted. "Dilly!"

He pressed his hands to his forehead. He thought he must be losing his senses from exhaustion. He could not see Dilly anywhere—nothing but the huge pond in the middle of the highway, the stalled cars, and now another semi slowly maneuvering through the bottleneck and thrusting out waves that rocked the cars and sloshed against his legs as he waded out to where he had last seen Dilly with his thumb stuck out.

"Dilly!" he called. "Where are you, Dilly?"

Had the boy returned to the car? Had he fallen asleep in there? That, Blackburn thought, was what must have happened. He turned back to the car, but Dilly was not there. He definitely, absolutely was not; but Blackburn had so convinced himself that that was where he would find him that, not believing the evidence of his own senses, he returned to the car again and again to look. What else could have happened? Could Dilly have gone over to play on the concrete barriers? Could he have gone off to the side of the highway to wait? Was it possible that, when he was standing out there trying to flag cars down, one of them had picked him up and he had gone off, looking for help, without letting Blackburn know?

But he already knew that none of those things was true.

*　　　*　　　*

The women did not arrive till after noon. They had taken a plane to Chicago, and from there a cab to the police station in

Vernal, where Blackburn, though he had been freed hours before, was still waiting for them. He had read the morning paper from start to finish, and now for some time he had been sitting on a yellow wooden bench and memorizing the pattern of black and white tiles on the station floor. When his wife came in, leaning on the shoulder of the neighbor who had accompanied her from Des Moines, Blackburn dropped his tired chewing gum into an ashtray and stood up. His wife put her face against his chest and said nothing.

The police had come to the flooded underpass at last after the reports of a couple of truckers who said their rigs had been attacked, as they drove through, by a man with a metal stanchion; he had been standing thigh-deep in the water, one of the drivers said, and he had been baying like a hound. The look of the man, the driver said, was frightening; it gave him the cold shivers. When the police came Blackburn was still there. He was standing silently in the cold dark water with the metal post from a no-parking sign clubbed in his hands, and when they approached him he began to babble incoherently about his son. The only way they could persuade him to come away was to shackle his hands behind his back. It was not until hours later, until two in the morning, after the traffic had finally been diverted from the highway and the pumpers had been sent out to siphon the water away from the underpass, that they found that he really had a son. It was not until then that they found the boy.

But now it was much later. It was after noon. The sunlight was beginning to slant through the high narrow windows behind Blackburn's wife, and when Blackburn placed a gentle kiss on her pale, damp forehead, she took hold of his hands and looked into his eyes dreamily. He knew she was still in shock. She was full of tranquilizers besides, and on the plane she had drunk two margaritas; without Mrs. Rose's shoulder to lean on she would have fallen flat on her face. Blackburn kissed her forehead again and then, as she still clung to his hands, muttered a few words of apology—apology for making her take the day off from work. He knew as soon as the words were out that it was not the right thing to say, but whatever the right thing was was still buried deep inside him; it would come out only bit by bit; it would seep out at times when he least expected it, and it would inundate the hours of his life; and never, never, in all the course of his life, would he ever be free of it again. But now it was all inside him still. He put his arm around his wife and then he looked at Mrs. Rose and put a hand on her shoulder and said, "Liz, it was so good of you to come." But everything else was hidden deep inside him. All he could think about was that his wife had had to take a day off from work. He felt apologetic about that, and he wanted her to understand how it had happened. He kept his arm around her and went out with her and Mrs. Rose to the cab they had taken from Chicago—the car had been towed to a service station in Hammond, and they would have to go get that, too, after they had done everything else they had to do.

They sat in the back of the cab, and Blackburn leaned forward to give the driver directions. "We'll go by where it happened," he told the women.

His wife, with a scarcely perceptible nod of her head, agreed, but Mrs. Rose was horrified.

"No. No," she said. "Good heavens, no—you don't want to see that."

"Don't you, honey?" Blackburn said.

Blackburn's wife looked blankly from Blackburn to Mrs. Rose. She looked out the window as Blackburn directed the cabby to the spot.

*   *   *

The cab drove slowly across the overpass, made a U-turn, and drove slowly back again. At the end of the overpass the cab stopped and Blackburn and his wife got out. She leaned on his arm and he walked her over to the rail.

"Honey, this is where it happened," he said, looking down at the freeway. "It was flooded, you see—"

She nodded. "Yes," she said.

"It was all covered in water," Blackburn said.

Hand in hand, they looked down on the freeway. It was dry now; the sun shone brightly and glinted against the glass and chrome of passing cars. There was no water on the freeway now and no sign that there had ever been water there. The traffic rolled along smoothly and looked as though it might continue unimpeded—through winter and summer, through day and night, through sunshine and through rain—for a thousand years.

Galb's Elbow

The girl is in the background, sitting on a blue suitcase with her eyes cast down demurely when Galb's van rattles past, but the man, standing in front of a big blinking yellow construction arrow, looks directly into Galb's eyes as if he knows that Galb is just exactly the person they've been waiting for. When Galb finally makes up his mind to pull over, he is half a mile down the road. But they have seen him stop; through the dusty rear window he can see them picking up their suitcases and trudging toward him slowly along the shoulder of the highway. Little spurts of dust rise from their feet. Galb switches the radio from classical to pop, then snaps it off and gets out of the van. He has not had anything to eat all morning, and now, waiting for the hitchhikers, he leans against one of the white posts that line the road and chews on a dry cheese sandwich.

According to the signs, he is almost at Memphis, and that means he should be in Shreveport by evening. And Shreveport means Marjorie. But Galb has been doing a lot of thinking during the past six hundred miles, and one of the things he has been thinking about is that Marjorie's letters have been getting colder and colder. And the last time he called her—why did she sound so perturbed?

The hitchhikers are getting closer, and Galb glances at them. The girl wears a light muslin shift and powder-blue denims. She has a round, placid face, and her sand-brown hair is tied at the back of her head. The man is smaller and broader than Galb, wearing an old navy shirt with a pair of chevrons on the shoulder and—though it is hot in the May sunshine—a wool watchcap on his head. He is grinning from ear to ear. Galb drops his eyes and concentrates on his cheese sandwich again.

It will be as it was with Aline, he thinks. Marjorie's eyes will be evasive. *John*, she will say, *John, I've been thinking things over, and . . . .*

Galb tosses the remainder of the sandwich into the weeds.

He gets himself a caffeine tablet from the box in the glove compartment. When the hitchhikers come up to the van the tablet is beginning to dissolve in his mouth, and his lips twist a little from the bitter taste.

"Howdy," says the man.

"Throw those in there," Galb says, pointing to the open side door.

The man shoves in the heavy tan suitcase first and then the little blue suitcase of the girl. The girl is already climbing into the front seat. Galb sees her in the corner of his eye while he washes down the remnants of the caffeine tablet with water from his canteen. He spits in the dust at the side of the road.

"Where you headed?" he asks the man.

"Texas. Dawg."

"Dawg? Is that in Texas?"

"Bout one hundred miles short of Dallas."

"I can take you as far as Jackson." He knows he will not feel like putting up with them all the way to Shreveport. Not even the two hundred miles to Jackson, for that matter—the name just popped into his head. Jackson is where Aline is living. "That's as far as I'm going," he says. "Jackson."

The girl is sitting on the uncomfortable middle seat, which is really just a folding stadium seat bolted to the engine cover, and when the man climbs in she whispers something in his ear.

". . . mmmb, Ricky?"

"Naw," Ricky says when she is through. He smirks, shakes his head, laughs. "*Naw.*"

Galb starts the engine. He swerves past another of the huge blinking yellow arrows and pulls out onto the highway. There is a construction project ahead.

"Honest to god," Ricky tells the girl loudly, "if you was any smarter we'd have to keep you tied up."

All the cars are being funneled into a single lane. A workman waves a red flag lethargically while half a dozen other workers sit around on lengths of sewer pipe and watch the traffic going by. Everything is covered with dust.

"You live down there? Down in Jackson?" Ricky says.

"I'm just—stopping to see a friend." A cattle truck swerves in front of him, and Galb eases his foot off the gas.

"*Look* at that bastard!" Ricky says.

For four years Galb did not even know where Aline had gone, but a couple of Christmases ago she sent him a photographic Christmas card from Jackson. She and a man with a black mustache were posed with two babies, a blurred dog, and a parakeet in a cage. Everybody except the parakeet had red eyes.

"What are you doing over there in Hawg?" Galb asks.

"Not *Hawg*," Ricky says. "That's in Looziana. Hell, I wouldn't live in Looziana if you paid me—specially not in Hawg! I'm talking about Texas, man! *Dawg*."

"Dawg," Galb says.

"I work the oilfields."

"Sounds interesting."

"It don't pay too bad, but it don't pay too good." Ricky lights a cigarette and breathes deep. "Galley work. You know what I mean?"

"Galley work?"

"Sure."

"Cooking, and . . . dishwashing?"

"Hell, I do everything. And if there ain't anything in the oilfield, I'll drive me a cab. It ain't too bad, but . . . ." Half of Ricky's words go out the window with his cigarette smoke. ". . . up to Grand City. That's where my old grammy lives. Been there ten months but I said the hell with it . . . ."

Whenever Ricky pauses, Galb makes noncommittal grunts to show that he is listening. The girl says nothing. She sits between them with her hands on her plump thighs and just keeps looking ahead at the highway.

"Take it or leave it, mister, I tell him. He says, Okay . . ."

The cattle truck takes one of the Memphis turnoffs and Ricky sticks out his finger at the driver.

"Why'd you leave Grand City?" Galb asks.

Ricky keeps on smoking, then stubs out his cigarette on the windshield and tosses it out the window. He elbows the girl in the ribs.

"Family difficulties," he says. It seems to be a private joke, but Galb laughs anyway.

"Anyplace there's a family there are family difficulties."

"*Haw*!" Ricky grunts. But the girl laughs, and Galb, though embarrassed, feels at the same time strangely proud that he has gotten through to her.

*   *   *

When Galb stops for gas, Ricky and the girl murmur together. Ricky pulls a battered wallet from his pocket and counts some money into her hand. She looks at him anxiously.

"Should I buy . . . the three-dollar box?"

"How you gonna buy anything else, when that's all we got!"

She goes bouncing across the road toward a restaurant featuring Dixie fried chicken. On the roof there is a mass of neon tubing depicting a giant hen holding the flag of the Confederacy. Galb, watching her horsetail of hair flipping back and forth, suddenly feels his heart go thump: there's something attractive about her. Ricky too is watching her, and when she disappears into the building he shakes his head like a worried parent.

"I swear to Jesus."

Galb pays the attendant and opens the engine cover to look at the oil. Everything is okay. He closes it up again and washes some of the dead bugs off the windshield. Ricky is leaning against one of the gasoline pumps, smoking.

"This person in Jackson, it's a girl I used to be engaged to," Galb says, wringing out the sponge.

"O yeh?"

"A grade-A bitch," Galb says.

Ricky inspects his cigarette. "How come you're going to see her if she's such a bitch?"

"I haven't seen her for a long time."

The girl is coming back, carrying a grease-stained box, and Ricky crushes out his cigarette. When they are out on the highway she opens the box. There are a few pieces of chicken, a roll, and a tiny container of coleslaw.

"I doan like that," she tells Ricky. "*You* have it."

Galb keeps his eyes on the highway and tries to avoid listen-

ing to them eat. Why did he confide in Ricky? Why did he say
something he did not even believe? Certainly he has never
thought of Aline as a grade-A bitch. She was never that at all.

After a while he hears Ricky sigh. Ricky tosses a couple of
bones out the window and wipes his hands on a tiny paper
napkin that begins to disintegrate immediately. He lights
another cigarette.

". . . saw me playing the machines, said Shit! Why ain't that
kid in school! So they call my dad. He says, Shit, the fucker got
hisself out there all right, let him get his ass back on home
again!"

The girl is so placid and quiet that Galb can picture her off in
a field somewhere, out in the green grass, swishing her little
tail of hair every now and then to keep the flies away. He holds
out a package of chewing gum.

"Want some?"

She takes a piece and crumples it into her mouth dreamily.
Ricky declines by whisking the air with his hand.

"Don't mind my smoking, do you?"

"No."

"Well, I'd done some penny-ante stuff before, but nothing
like that. He hoists me through the window . . . ."

The snap of chewing gum drowns out some of the details,
but Galb is envious anyway. He has not had a very adven-
turesome life.

"Turns out he didn't know a flea's ass about safecracking. We
bust open a candy machine and get maybe thirty dollars in
nickels and dimes. He was so mad! He starts cramming candy
and bubblegum into his mouth, he fills his pockets with chocolate and jujubes, the damn fool . . . . Halfway into town we
get stopped by the cops, and they think, Hmmm—what's this!
Candy and money falling out of all his pockets, chocolate
smeared all over his face. That stupid fart—they sent him to
the big rock candy mountain. Not me . . . ."

"But—"

". . ."

Ricky sinks down in the seat and seems to be sleeping. The
girl keeps chewing her gum. What is she thinking about? Galb
wonders. Is she thinking about anything?

Tall pines border one side of the highway, casting cool shadows onto the concrete and filling the air with their scent. On the other side are fields. The sky is vast and blue, dotted with occasional puffs and rags of clouds.

Suddenly a blue jay comes winging heedlessly across the road like somebody's lost paper airplane. Galb jerks the wheel ineffectually—too late. The jay smacks into the front of the van, *thump!*, and tumbles to the pavement.

"Shit."

"Ya got him!" Ricky says cheerfully.

Galb grits his teeth. The girl, he thinks, must be embarrassed. She is tied to Ricky by her passiveness and timidity, but she is constantly offended by Ricky's gauche, insulting ways.

"A blue jay," Ricky adds in a moment. "Them's pretty birds."

"Quite," Galb says.

A tiny smile on the girl's face. On the other side of her, by the window, Ricky is closing his eyes again. He folds his arms across his chest and sinks down in the seat with his chin resting on his collarbone.

"There's a mattress back there," Galb points out.

"Well, hell," Ricky says. He clambers over the back of the seat and collapses onto the mattress. "Ahhh . . ."

Instead of moving over to the more comfortable seat Ricky has vacated, the girl, to Galb's surprise, remains glued to the makeshift seat on the engine cover, which is small and hard. Does she think it would be impolite for her to move? Is she afraid to offend Ricky by taking his seat? Galb glances at her, but that tells him nothing. She is chewing her gum placidly and looking straight ahead at the road.

"Not the most comfortable seat in the world," he says.

She does not reply, but her face breaks into a great beaming smile, as though she believes his words to have been extremely clever and amusing. This reaction embarrasses Galb.

"*I* wouldn't want to sit there," he says, more to himself than to her.

He tries to concentrate on his driving, but now the girl is in his mind and he can't seem to get her out. Could it be that she is staying on the seat next to his because she is attracted to him? He immediately discounts this possibility, but he cannot stop thinking about it. His eyes dart to the convex rearview mirror, which gives him a slight, distorted image of his face. Some women have thought him handsome. The black tennis jersey he is wearing now is the one he had on when Marjorie told him he was a fox, a definite fox, in black. Then too there is his manner, an air of erudition which has been very appealing to a certain type of woman . . .

Galb has become so caught up in his impersonal analysis of the situation that it comes as a shock for him to realize that his elbow is beginning to rub against the girl's hip every time he moves the steering wheel. Did he move closer, or did she? After a few minutes she moves away slightly, and Galb tells himself he was imagining things. She turns around and looks into the back, as if checking on a sleeping child. Galb also glances back, but the curtain has been pulled, and he can't see. Did she pull the curtain over? The curtain is of a loose enough weave that you can peer through it if you try—and that may be what Ricky is doing right now, sitting back there and peering through and seeing everything that's going on.

Now she is suddenly close against him again, and for a moment the van veers into the other lane. Galb brings it back with his left hand. His right hand rests only lightly on the wheel; he is doing all the steering with his left so that his right arm will be free to move, within a certain circumscribed area, where it will. His elbow touches her waist and then, caressing, drops to the curve of her hip. It lingers there awhile and then moves lower and begins to probe, like the nose of a friendly hound, at the juncture of her hip and thigh. Galb's face is flushed. The van veers across the white line again and he thinks he must be going crazy. He will die in a fiery crash on the Mississippi highway, and no one will ever know, as they stand weeping over his tomb, that John Galb was killed by his elbow's lust.

Surely, he tells himself, the girl is not really permitting him to take these liberties. Surely she must believe all these touches to be accidental. Galb's head is throbbing. He wrestles with his thoughts. Is she really responding, or is it all only in his mind? It must be only in his mind—but even so, he can restrain himself no longer. His right hand, shaking with trepidation, slides from the steering wheel and falls onto her thigh.

For a moment it just lies there, like a stray, windblown leaf. The girl gives no sign that she is aware of its presence. She will not encourage it perhaps, but she will not brush it away either. Galb understands the rules immediately: she will do nothing, but he is permitted to do whatever he wants. His fingers touch the inside of her thigh, and a car roars by outside, its horn blaring. Galb corrects his steering once again. His fingers move along her thigh like itsy-bitsy spiders . . . Suddenly she turns her head, and Ricky pushes through the curtains. Galb's hand is back on the steering wheel so fast it might never have left.

"Hot back there?"

"It weren't so bad."

Ricky is grinning, but his grin appears to have no significance. The girl, however, looks as though she has just swallowed a whole mouthful of laughter and is on the verge of exploding with it. Her eyes are bright, her cheeks are pink, her lips are quivering—but she keeps it all in.

"Wasn't really sleeping," Ricky says. "Just sort of lying there. We was in this motel last night and we got a lot of sleep." He yawns and lights a cigarette. "Whyn't you go back there and sleep for a while?" he asks the girl.

"You slept enough for both of us!" She lets out a brief, spasmodic laugh.

"I don't get the joke, but I guess you don't feel like sleeping."

The girl gives another choked laugh, and Ricky looks out the window. A big green sign at the side of the road tells the distances to Jackson, Vicksburg, and New Orleans. "What the hell, we're almost to Jackson already anyway." He shifts in his seat and pulls some crumpled pieces of an old map from his hind pocket. "This is how we got to go," he tells the girl, balancing the pieces on his knee. She leans toward him, following his moving finger, and at the same time her calf presses against Galb's.

"You getting off the highway this side of Jackson or the other side of Jackson?" Ricky asks. "Or are you going right on into downtown Jackson?"

"Listen, maybe I won't even stop in Jackson after all," Galb says, returning the pressure of her calf. "I don't know *what* I'm doing."

*   *   *

He stops at a shopping center north of the city and the sun beats down on his shoulders while he looks up Aline's number at an open telephone outside the discount drugstore. There is an irresistible smell of broiling steak from an unseen restaurant or from someone's backyard grill. He finds her number in the book and underlines it, but he is hesitant about calling. What can he say to her after all these years?

He looks over at the van. The hitchhikers are sitting inside, waiting for him. At last he dials the number, and the telephone rings again and again—six times, seven times, eight times. As he is about to hang up, she answers. He would know her voice anywhere.

"Hello," she says. "Hello? . . . Is anybody there?"

He doesn't take the phone from his ear, but he touches the cradle lightly and breaks the connection. He closes his eyes and listens: he can hear the sounds of the highway still, and he can hear children and shoppers, and he can hear the sound of wind in the high tops of trees. In a moment a slight breeze, filled with dust and heat, brushes his cheeks, and Galb opens his eyes again.

Down the arcade, in front of the grocery store, two little kids are climbing on a mechanical horse which is supposed to jiggle when a coin is inserted behind the right ear. Somebody has written "Out of order" on its saddle in smeary red lipstick, and the kids are getting it all over them.

He rubs his eyes briefly, then empties his purse onto the little shelf beneath the telephone and counts out the money to call Shreveport. Marjorie answers immediately.

"John! What's wrong, are you okay? Where are you?"

"No, I just thought I'd call and say hello."

"Well, hel*lo*," she says. "Hello."

Her voice is like the aroma of that broiling steak. It is delectable but insubstantial, and it touches a hunger he did not know was there.

"Honey, I think I'll be there in about four hours."

"Four *hours*! Well, but—?"

"I'm in Jackson," he says.

"Jackson! Jackson?"

Somebody has left the stub of a pencil on the shelf and, as he talks, Galb marks crosshatches and curlicues on the gray painted metal.

"I just thought I'd warn you I was on my way."

"Darling, there are lots of things we have to talk about."

"Yes," Galb says. "I know."

He glances over at his van, gleaming in the sunlight. Ricky is standing outside, looking off toward a watertower that rises above the pines. The girl is still inside.

"Then, well, I'll see you tonight," Marjorie says.

"This evening."

"Yes," she says. "I'll see you this evening."

Among his doodlings on the shelf Galb has written "Love," and when he puts the phone down he draws a big, lopsided heart around the word. Then he scratches out the whole mess and goes back to the van.

"Listen," he says, pulling out of the parking lot, "I'm not going to stop in Jackson. I'm going to drive on to Shreveport. I know this person I can stay with in Shreveport."

Ricky is using his teeth to tear the cellophane wrapper from a cigarette package. The cellophane flies out the window.

"I mean, if you want a ride," Galb says.

"Great," Ricky says. "Shreveport. Hell, that's practically shouting distance from Dawg. We're gonna get home by dark."

The girl is still chewing the gum Galb gave her hours ago. She presses her leg against his.

". . . back to Dawg tonight and I'll be driving the cab. Just hope Miz Markey still has that trailer—whoops!"

The van begins shaking from a series of cracks and bumps in the road, and Ricky says something about the politicians.

"Sure," Galb says.

". . . just interested in plastering their own little nest, but who blames them? Hell, I'd be doing the same damn thing."

"Who wouldn't?"

"Got a trailer we was renting from Miz Markey. If Bob's still there we'll move in with him. He might have gone to Atlanta but I don't think so . . . ."

*   *   *

Galb stops for gas again across the river. Ricky gets out and goes off to the row of candy and cigarette machines inside the building, and Galb turns to the girl, intending to kiss her.

"Premium?" the acned attendant asks, peering in the window.

"Regular."

The girl climbs down and takes the box the fried chicken came in over to a trashcan. Galb follows her over. Behind the plate glass he can see Ricky still deliberating over the candies and cigarettes.

She finds one piece that has not been thoroughly chewed and stands by the trashcan, peeling the meat off delicately with her teeth. When she drops the bone into the trash her lips and fingers are shiny with grease, but to Galb that does not lessen her attractiveness at all—it actually seems to render her infinitely more appealing. With his heart in his mouth, Galb steps closer.

"I forgot to ask," the attendant says. "Did you want it filled up?"

"Yes," Galb says. "Fill it up."

Now Ricky is coming back, unwrapping a big brown candy bar and grinning as he steps out of the gas station. Galb crosses the baking asphalt and lets himself into the cool, concrete-floored restroom at the side of the building. The lock is broken. He leans against the door to keep it firmly shut, and reaches beneath his waistband, where he has a moneybelt containing five crisp pieces of currency. He transfers one of the pieces to his wallet, and he is tucking the moneybelt out of sight again just as somebody tries the door and knocks.

"Anybody in there?" It's Ricky.

"Wait a minute." Galb flushes the toilet and goes out.

"Didn't know no one was in there," Ricky calls after him. "Hell, you can finish up with what you was doing."

The girl is sitting on the step of the van, licking chocolate from her fingers. Galb opens the side door and looks into his cooler.

"I've got some hard-boiled eggs in there," he tells her.

"I doan like eggs."

"There's some milk, too."

"I doan like milk."

"Here's some dry-roasted peanuts."

"I *like* nuts."

Galb hands her the jar. She gives it a try, then hands it back for him to open. She takes a modest handful, and as she is sitting there eating them, one at a time, out of her palm, Galb opens his wallet and shows her the money. She looks at the money and then she looks at Galb.

"It's a hunerd dollars!"

"Do you want it?"

"Are you fooling?"

"Take it," he says. "It's for you."

She holds out the hundred-dollar bill and squints at it, but then, as Ricky comes out of the restroom, she folds it up into a tiny square and pats it into her back pocket.

"Can I have some more of those nuts?"

One of the attendants is running a hose on the pavement, and he turns it down when Ricky crosses to the van. The water steams off almost as soon as it hits the blacktop.

"Ahhh," Ricky says, rubbing his groin. "I needed that real bad. You want to change seats for a while?"

The girl mulls over his offer while she finishes her peanuts. At last she agrees to change places. Ricky sits on the hard little seat in the middle, and the girl sits over by the window. Galb feels bereft.

"Should have told me if your behind was getting sore," Ricky tells her. "Hell, I would have traded with you."

She just smiles and looks out the window.

"She's the only one who's ever sat there without complaining how uncomfortable it was," Galb tells Ricky.

"She never says anything." Ricky sounds puzzled and a little annoyed. "Never says a thing."

*　　　*　　　*

The last miles to Shreveport are passed in silence. Galb is driving into the sun, and the glare is hard on his eyes. He's tired. When he sees the sign marking Shreveport's outer limit, he slows down.

"How far on is Dawg?"

"Probly bout one hundred miles," says Ricky. "Be there fore it gets dark."

"Sort of feel as though I ought to drive you on over there," Galb says, "but . . ."

He is tempted to do it; he would do it without question if, when they got there, Ricky would say, Hell, come on in and stay the night!

"If I knew anyone there, had a place to stay, I'd do it. Maybe look around Dawg a little. Much to do around there?"

"Well, it's a nice place," Ricky says warily. "Most anything you want to do, you can do in Dawg."

It ain't much, Galb imagines Ricky saying, but we always got room on the floor! And then Ricky would go out and drive his cab or drink with the boys awhile—You keep Mister Galb company, will you, honey?—and leave Galb alone with the girl in that dingy furnished trailer of Miz Markey's.

"Yes, if I had a place to stay tonight, I'd drive you right over. Don't think I know anyone in Dawg . . ."

But he can see that Ricky is not listening. Ricky is not aware of the possibilities at all.

"Here we are," he says, pulling over at the last moment before the final Shreveport exit. "Far as I'm going."

The three of them climb out and Ricky drags out the suitcases. The girl takes the blue one. She grasps the handle with both hands and the suitcase hangs down against her thighs. Her eyes wander off to the side of the highway, into the tops of trees and the roofs of houses.

"Hate to put you out on the road," Galb says.

"Hell, we preciate your taking us this far!"

"Well, maybe I'll get over to Dawg in a day or two. Stop in at your trailer with a sixpack or something."

The girl still doesn't look at him. Ricky holds out his hand.

"That'd be real nice. Just ask about me at the cab company. Just ask for Ricky. They'll know where I am."

He and Galb press their hands together warmly.

When Galb drives away down the off-ramp, he can see them in his rearview mirror: Ricky with his watchcap low on his forehead and his thumb stuck out, and the girl, behind him, sitting on her blue suitcase.

"Dear Jesus," he whispers. "Sweet Jesus Christ."

    *   *   *

Much later that night, in the lilac-scented darkness of Marjorie's room, Galb wakes from a bad dream and cannot get to sleep again. The dream was of Marjorie. He dreamed they were traveling together with a couple of other people—the hitchhikers? her parents?—and after driving away from a gas station he realized he had left her behind. But he couldn't go back; according to the logic of the dream, that going-away was irreversible and forever.

She is curled beside him in the bed, with her back to him, sleeping—a small, dark woman whose beauty and caring and intelligence have always amazed and gratified him. She is everything to him. Why, then, does he wish her gone? Why does he yearn instead for a dry little town in Texas, a rented trailer, and the hitchhiker's gum-chewing, inarticulate blond in his arms?

Why? Why? Unable to sleep, Galb mouths these questions silently; but the answers, if there are any, are lost in the surrounding dark.

Waterlilies

While he tried to explain to Lena where the bus had let him off (through the dirty window of the Amgas station he could see, on the other side of a slushy main street, a Shur-Save market and a theater) Brueggeman drew cartoon planets and stars and Ignatz the mouse on the back of the photo she'd sent.

"I don't know what *street*," he said, "but I'm right across from a movie theater, a big orange building—the Berky Rialto. Know where that is?"

"The Berky Rialto? I can't think—"

He drew a box around her phone number on the back of the photo, then turned the box into a brick that was hurtling through the air.

"O, *South* Westham!" she said at last. "O no, no, you should have stayed on and gotten off at Westham *Corners*, but that's all right, that's all right—I'll come down for you, Pootzie and I!"

When she hung up he leaned against the cigarette machine, looking at the photo and wondering what he was letting himself in for. The photo wasn't of her, but of the portrait he'd done of her eleven years before, when she was twenty-one. It showed a small beautiful woman with intense bright eyes and an overwhelming smile. It was very good work—probably the best portrait he'd ever done.

He put the photo away and waited.

*   *   *

After half an hour a small yellow car, driven by a petite, dark-haired woman, pulled into the station, and Brueggeman picked up his suitcase and went outside.

But the car pulled up beside a pump, and the driver, getting out to fill her tank, gave Brueggeman only a cursory glance. Brueggeman stopped and put down his suitcase. While he was still trying to decide whether it was possible that she could be Lena, another car pulled up beside him, this one an old blue clunker with a crushed passenger door and fenders eaten through with rust—and from the smile on the face of the woman inside, Brueggeman knew, without actually recognizing her, that this must be Lena. She had turned into a middle-aged fat woman. "Sorry I kept you waiting," she said, climbing heavily out of the car.

A large hairy red dog bounded over the seatback and squeezed past her. It bounded through the slush, clawed its way up the front of Brueggeman's coat, and smacked its long wet tongue against his chin.

"Down, Pootzie," she said. She smiled as Brueggeman retreated and tried to brush the muddy footprints off his coat. "Pootzie always gets so excited around people." She attached the dog to a leash and began to lead it toward a snowbank at the rear of the gas station. "You don't mind, do you?" she said. "He hasn't been out all day, poor dear. We'll just be a moment. Go ahead and throw your suitcase into the car."

Brueggeman picked up his suitcase, but then did not move. He watched her following her dog around, waiting for it to relieve itself in the snow, and tried to reconcile this image with the one he had in his mind. She had changed so drastically that he felt like throwing himself down in the snow and weeping.

Her voice was the same sensuous contralto it had always been, but everything else was gone. She had been tiny. When he did her portrait it was on an enormous canvas, a canvas that reached almost from floor to ceiling, so as to emphasize her tininess. The background had been big and gray like the gray of summer thunderclouds, and light had flowed from her as from a diamond. Light had flashed from her intense dark eyes. Light had shone from her bright, inquisitive, smiling mouth. There had been light on her legs, on her bare feet. Her frilly white Victorian blouse had been a pool of light. Her tiny chin, her cheekbones, the bridge of her nose all had cupped the light.

But now it all was gone. She had been so lovely—so soft, so young, so shining, so small—but everything, now, was gone.

"Try over here, Pootzie," she told the dog.

Everything seemed to have been submerged beneath a great tide of fat. Her cheekbones had disappeared and her chin

was a tiny bubble of fat and her nose had metamorphosed into
a piece of shiny pink flotsam. Her eyes, which had been dark
and shining like the eyes of a small bright bird, were hidden
now behind a pair of cheap black-rimmed glasses that made
her look like a sad immigrant anarchist. And even her hair,
which had been so long and thick, which he had delighted in
running his fingers through, had been terribly desecrated: it
had been chopped short and pasted into tiny ringlets that lay
so close to her skull that areas of pallid scalp shone out
between. How could she have done that to her beautiful hair?
Now it did not look like hair at all, Brueggeman thought, but
like a doily crocheted out of shiny black yarn.

Lena saw him staring at her and smiled. "Do your business,
Pootzum," she told the dog. "We haven't got all day."

Brueggeman turned and threw his suitcase into the car.

*   *   *

He kept his arm up, on the drive to her apartment complex,
to discourage Pootzie from leaping over the seatback and onto
his lap, as the dog appeared to be preparing to do, and he
opened the window a crack to try to dissipate the smell of wet
dog and the smoke from Lena's cigarette, which were making
him nauseous. At a stoplight near the campus, Lena turned to
him and smiled.

"Well, we've got more gray hairs than we used to, but I
guess we don't really look that much different."

Brueggeman felt himself blushing, embarrassed for her.

"If I saw you on the street," he said cautiously, "I wouldn't
recognize you."

"Really? You wouldn't?"

"Maybe it's your glasses. Of course you didn't use to smoke.
Your hair is different."

She rolled down her window and tossed out the stub of her
cigarette. "I guess I've gained some weight since I knew you."

"Maybe that's it."

"*You* certainly haven't changed."

When she pulled in at Hollypark Gardens the dog put its
forepaws on the seatback and began to moan softly. After kill-

ing the engine Lena rubbed the dog's ears for a moment and smiled at Brueggeman.

"Anyway, it doesn't matter what we look like on the outside. We're still the same people on the inside, aren't we?"

"I guess we are."

Her apartment was a one-bedroom one, which she shared with the dog and three cats, on the second floor. When she opened the door Pootzie lunged toward one of the cats, a big black-and-white male that had paused in the middle of the living room to wrestle with a flea, and tried to mount him. With a hiss of annoyance, the cat dragged himself free and leaped onto a bookcase. Lena, thrusting her black fur coat onto a hook on the back of the closet door, clicked her tongue disparagingly at Pootzie and then turned to Brueggeman.

"Want something to eat?"

"No."

"Why don't you throw your things in the bedroom?"

She went into the kitchen. Through the bedroom wall Brueggeman could hear the water splashing and the plates clinking and Lena humming to herself while she washed the dishes.

He put down his suitcase beside the bed. A fluffy gray cat was asleep on the pink quilt. Brueggeman looked out the window. Between the apartment buildings there was a gray wooden fence against which lay a rusting bike frame. Beyond the fence he saw a dumpster, and beyond that a small slide and a couple of swings, one of which had a broken seat. He turned back into the bedroom. Lena had a few photos on the wall, and one of these, in an ornate gilt frame above the marble-topped bureau, Brueggeman looked at for some time. It showed a little girl of about six, her hair in bangs, wading in a stream—Lena herself, he supposed. She was smiling, but her eyes, it seemed to him, reflected a secret sadness. Beneath this photo, in a little jar on the bureau, were some broken flower petals intermixed with what looked like bits of tea and spices; next to it, in a pink glass candy dish shaped like a scallop shell, there were three or four foil-wrapped condoms.

As he left the room the cat stretched and yawned and then, making its paws into little fists, curled up to sleep some more.

Pootzie peered out from beneath the living room coffee table and thumped his tail on the carpet when Brueggeman passed by. Lena was still in the kitchen washing dishes.

"Unfortunately I'm not going to be able to stay as long as I'd hoped," Brueggeman said. "There's one sort of semiconceptual piece I've been working on—"

"The one with the weather balloons and the pigeons?"

Again he felt himself blushing. He had had the foresight, when he talked to her on the telephone the week before about coming up, to mention the piece as a reason he might have to leave early. But now, in her company, the very idea of it embarrassed him.

"It's probably a piece of shit," he said, "but it's driving me crazy. I'm going to have to go back tomorrow and see what I can do with it."

Lena came out from the kitchen, wiping her hands on a scrap of towel.

"That's not so terrible, is it? At least we get a *little* visit. Maybe we can have a longer visit in the spring."

She sat down in a green chintz easychair at the end of the room and, as she lit herself a cigarette, the dog came over to bury its snout beneath her breast. Brueggeman stood looking out the window—a broad window framed by spider plants and pink begonias, some of them hanging from the ceiling in macrame slings, others resting on a bookcase beneath. The window looked out on the slushy parking lot between the white brick buildings of Hollypark Gardens, a few skeletal trees, and, in the far distance, the purple-gray silhouettes of the Berkshires. An orange cat lay between a couple of the plants on the bookcase. Brueggeman scratched its head and it began to purr.

"I came across some of your old letters the other day," Lena said.

"You kept my letters?"

"Sure. All of them. I won't ask if you kept mine, cause I never sent you any." She laughed. "They were nice letters—all so full of love."

Brueggeman picked up the cat and began to stroke it. He remembered the letters very well. They were full of youthful intensity and hyperbole. A dozen times, while he was still living with Miriam, he had used the postal system to send Lena promises of his undying love.

"In one of them you said you wanted me to have your child. Do you remember that?"

"Vaguely."

"That was a nice letter."

"Was it?"

"You probably had it mimeographed and sent it to all your girlfriends."

"Sure. But I didn't get too many takers."

"Only Miriam," Lena said.

That was supposed to be a harmless little joke, Brueggeman knew, but it scraped up a memory that was still excruciating for him. He and Miriam had had a baby, but it had died at birth. It had never even had a name. At the burial site in California it was identified only as Baby Girl Brueggeman. Had Lena never known about that?

"That's right," he said. "Miriam was the only one."

"It was a beautiful letter anyway, mimeographed or not. You wrote me such a lot of letters. I always wanted to write you back but I kept thinking if you got a letter from me Miriam would somehow know everything. But she wouldn't have, would she?"

"No."

"Did she ever guess about us?"

"No."

"Did you ever tell her?"

"No." He closed his eyes. He could see himself writing that letter. He was sitting in the little one-room apartment over the karate shop in Berkeley. He could see the sun shining in, the sunlight on her portrait (he had brought it west with him, thinking it not quite finished), the sunlight on the table where he tried to write to her, the sunlight on his cup of cold coffee. There was so much sunlight in that apartment. And Miriam loved him so. He was trying to live, trying to paint, trying to make some sort of future for himself and for Miriam, and all the time he kept thinking of Lena. Miriam could not have helped knowing about Lena, but she had kept it to herself. She had loved him, but to Brueggeman that had not seemed enough; nothing had seemed enough; he longed for Lena.

He opened his eyes and looked at her. Smoke drifted from her nose and hung above her head like a miniature cirrus cloud. Was this the woman who had filled his dreams?

"You hungry yet?"

"A little."

"I'll make you a sandwich."

On the wall over the green chair were some photos and cheap reproductions of paintings, and Brueggeman looked them over while Lena pulled sandwich materials out of her refrigerator. His own etching of Miriam, which he had sent as a sort of Christmas card six years before, hung next to a Rubens of a woman's face, pinkish and plump and full of bourgeois charm. A framed crayon drawing by a child. A Dali limp watch. Beneath the Dali, a photo of Lena as she used to be, with her hair still long and full, and the same intense beauty to her face that there had been when Brueggeman knew her. She was on a bench on a platform somewhere, waiting for a train. The photo was a lovely observation of forms, a lovely study of masses of dark and light.

"Mazurski took that," Lena said, seeing him looking at the photo.

Brueggeman went over to the dining alcove and watched as she slapped a sandwich together on the card table. She told him about Mazurski. He was a man she had lived with for four years, she said, before he suddenly walked out on her and got married to a stripper who called herself the Nicaraguan Bombshell.

"Married her three weeks later! Can you believe it?" Lena laughed. She licked some mayonnaise from the knife, cut the sandwich in two, and slid the plate across the table to Brueggeman. "He must have been cheating on me for months, the bastard! What a bastard he was."

The sandwich was full of Swiss cheese and salami and tomato slices and onions, all on heavy dark rye, and Lena brought out a beer from the refrigerator and poured it into a tall glass for Brueggeman.

"You still love him," Brueggeman said.

"Sure—who could resist a bastard like that?" She sat down across from him and smiled. "Eat," she said.

"How about you? You're not eating?"

"I don't eat lunch as a rule."

"You don't?"

"Go ahead—eat."

Brueggeman started in on the sandwich. Lena watched him eat and so did Pootzie, who was crouched under the table with his tongue hanging out and his tail beating the floor.

"If I eat lunch my stomach swells up. My shrink thought maybe it was because I wanted to get pregnant."

Brueggeman laughed. "The psychiatrist strikes again!"

"It was just something he threw out." Bending forward, she scooped the fluffy gray cat into her arms and began to pet it.

"*Do* you want to be pregnant?"

Brueggeman did not mean this question to be serious—it was merely an invitation to Lena to join him in a laugh at psychiatrists, whom he thought of as the fuddled men he had seen in urbane cartoons. But Lena took it seriously. She did not answer directly but, continuing to stroke the cat, told Brueggeman she thought maybe she was too old, maybe she was actually going through an early menopause—her periods had been irregular recently and a couple of black hairs had sprouted from her chin. Anyway, she said, she was afraid that if she were to have a child maybe she would tend to neglect it as she neglected, sometimes, Pootzie and the cats.

"Isn't that right, Lulabelle?" she asked the cat.

The doctor was absolutely right, Brueggeman understood; she did want to become pregnant. And suddenly he realized—putting together what she'd said about his letter with the shy sad way she was looking at him now—that it wasn't merely the abstract possibility of pregnancy that she was thinking about; what she was thinking about was the desirability of getting pregnant by him.

The dog leaned forward, while Brueggeman's mind was occupied with these other matters, and lifted the remainder of his sandwich neatly out of his hand. He gulped it down while Brueggeman looked on in amazement, then thumped his tail

on the floor a few times and deposited his chin on Brueggeman's thigh.

"Son of a bitch," Brueggeman said.

"He sure likes *you* all right," Lena said. "Pootzie knows he's
got a friend."

*   *   *

Eight years before, in the summer after Miriam had lost the
baby, they had journeyed east to forget about it. They made it a
long, leisurely trip, up along the coast and across Canada,
camping out and seeing old friends along the way, and with
them, all the way from Hollywood, they had brought, as a sort
of surrogate love-object, a little kitten named Sunshine.

Now, finishing his beer in the living room while Lena put-
tered about in the kitchen, Brueggeman remembered how
much he had wanted to get in touch with her that summer. He
had not seen her in three years, and all that time he had
believed he was in love with her. As soon as they got to Boston
he began to look for her. He followed her to one defunct
address after another, from Jamaica Plain to Somerville to Rox-
bury, but always she was gone.

Finally, at the end of a week, he got in touch with her, but
then it was too late. One of the people he had left a message
with came through, and Lena called him at Daniel's the last
day they were there. But it was too late; they were preparing to
leave Boston then, and a thunderstorm was brewing outside,
and everything seemed to be falling apart, and Lena was the
last person in the world he felt like seeing.

They had been staying in Daniel's living room for a week,
Miriam and he, and even though Daniel had said nothing they
knew they had outstayed their welcome. They had had to stay
because of the kitten. She had traveled with them for two
months and seven thousand miles, but when they reached
Boston she became sick. She would not eat. She looked at
Brueggeman with her trusting yellow eyes and made little
sounds of complaint, and he could do nothing for her. Miriam
cuddled her as they drove her down to the animal hospital,

and every day after that they went to see her in her little cage, but the experience was heartrending. She was not getting any better. Finally that morning the people from the animal hospital called him and told him she had died in the middle of the night. Brueggeman had not wept when they lost the baby, but when the kitten died he broke down, in front of Daniel, in tears. And when Lena called, late in that afternoon, he had nothing to say to her. He wondered what he had ever had to say to her, and he thought he would never have anything to say to her ever again. All he could think about then was getting out. They left Boston that night in a terrible thunderstorm. They drove only as far as Taunton, and there, alone with Miriam, for two days he did nothing but paint waterlilies, ten or fifteen or twenty expressionist pond pictures on gessoed boards—so that even now, it seemed to Brueggeman, if he were to see a waterlily his heart would become inflamed with sorrow: sorrow for the dead kitten, sorrow for Lena, and sorrow for their little unnamed darling who died at the moment of her birth, thanks to the fumbling of an inept frau doktor out in Hollywood. And sorrow that everything between Miriam and him had turned into dust.

Lena stood in the doorway and smiled at him. "What are you thinking?"

"Nothing."

"Nothing?" She kept smiling at him.

Brueggeman shook his head and rose from the chair. "I've been sitting around too much. Let's go out and do something."

*   *   *

There was a good Chinese restaurant Lena knew about, but when the food was already on the table she decided she weighed too much; she picked at her rice with the chopsticks and ate next to nothing. "You eat," she said. "I'm going to go on a diet for you. I'm too fat. The next time you see me I want to be thin."

But on the way back from the restaurant, seeing ahead the giant pink neon sign for Doobie's Donuts, she began to hum and to look at Brueggeman coyly, as if they shared a private joke.

"*Mmmmm,*" she said. "Wouldn't you just *love* a nice choco-late-covered doughnut now?"

Brueggeman said that he would not.

"No? You wouldn't? Fresh from the oven?"

As far as he knew, she had eaten nothing all day except three sweet-and-sour shrimps, a little egg foo yung, and a fortune cookie. No wonder she was hungry. "If you want one," he said, "why don't we stop?"

"Mmm," she said, rolling her eyes. "Ahhh."

"Well, let's get a doughnut."

"No no no," she said. "I was just joking, can't you tell? I don't really want a doughnut. Unless *you* do."

"Okay," Brueggeman said. "Yeh. Let's get one."

They had already driven past the place, but Lena did a fast U-turn and pulled up in front. "These are just going to be for you," she told Brueggeman before removing her key from the ignition. "Don't let me eat any of them."

Brueggeman shrugged. He was full of Chinese food, and as far as he was concerned the doughnuts were going to be for nobody else but her. And why shouldn't she have a doughnut? But obviously for Lena doughnuts had some meaning that they did not have for him.

As he stood beside her inside the shop he saw her eyes going rapidly back and forth across the racks of doughnuts. Her face and hands seemed to become red with gluttony when she held her ten-dollar bill out to the acned boy behind the counter. Brueggeman, embarrassed, turned and looked out the win-dow at the traffic.

"That crunchy kind there," Lena told the boy. "A half-dozen of those, and a half-dozen of the chocolate glazed ones, and I guess a dozen of those—those cream-filled ones."

The boy rapidly filled two boxes with doughnuts.

"Any blueberry ones?" she asked.

"These ones here are blueberries."

"A half-dozen of those."

Brueggeman carried the three boxes out to the car in silence.

"These are for you," she said, driving homeward. "I'm not going to eat a single one."

Brueggeman, holding the boxes between his lap and his

chin, did not reply. When they came back to her apartment he set the boxes down on her card table.

"Remember," Lena said, "they're all yours. Don't let me have any."

He turned away. He was certain she was going to wind up eating every one of the doughnuts.

"What?" she said. "What's the matter?"

"I'm not going to eat those doughnuts."

"You're not? Why not? What's wrong?"

"You think I'm going to eat two and a half dozen doughnuts?"

"You don't have to eat all of them."

"Who *is* going to eat all of them?"

"You can take the extras back to New York with you. You can share them with your friends. Can't you?"

Brueggeman picked up the black-and-white cat and began to pet it. Was it possible that he had misjudged her motivations? That she really had bought the doughnuts only for him?

"I just thought you might like them," she said. "Should we just throw them out? Maybe I did the wrong thing. Maybe you just don't like doughnuts."

He turned to her with a forced smile. "That was very thoughtful of you. I do like doughnuts. I'm just not terrifically hungry right now."

"God, I am," Lena said. "I could eat a whole dozen of them. If you see me anywhere near them, just beat me back with a stick."

*   *   *

Lena was staring at the television and humming something from Puccini. Brueggeman passed her the joint that he seemed to have been holding for a long time.

"You wanted to become an opera singer," he said.

"Me? Never."

"You said you did."

"If I did I was never serious about it."

She inhaled and closed her eyes and held the joint, glowing, at her fingertips. On the screen there were pictures of a bombing somewhere at the eastern end of the Mediterranean. A Semitic woman was squatting in the ashes that used to be her home, wailing and tearing at her face with her fingernails. Her husband and her babies had died in flames. For a moment Brueggeman watched in awe.

"Sure you were," he told Lena. "You were serious about it. Most serious thing in the world."

He reached out and managed to snag the joint again, but then it rolled out of his fingers and fell to the carpet. He rubbed his fingers across the carpet in search of it.

"Serious thing in the world?" she sighed.

"Probably chocolate-covered doughnuts," Brueggeman said. He found the joint and touched it to his lips again. Lena opened her eyes and looked at him.

"Is that what you said? Did you say chocolate-covered doughnuts? Did you say that?"

He shook his head. There wasn't anything left of the joint so he began to roll another on the back of an album cover.

"I should get up and switch to something else," she said.

The news had gone off and a movie had begun.

"This looks terrible," she said.

"Look at that!" A pterodactyl flew across the screen. Brueggeman laughed.

"Doesn't this look terrible?"

"It really looks bad."

The pterodactyl made a coughing sound, and Brueggeman laughed again and imitated the sound of the pterodactyl. He lit the joint and passed it to Lena. For a while they watched the gray flickering images on the screen in silence. It was a monster movie from Mexico. Tyrannosaurus Rex, looking disconcerted and rather lonely, was wandering through a Mexican marketplace, knocking over a stall here and an old pickup truck there like a child kicking a tin can. People screamed and crossed themselves. Grapefruits and pottery rolled in the dust.

"Jesus," Brueggeman said, "what a terrible movie. It's terrible."

"We're going to have bad dreams."

When the advertisement came on, Lena disappeared into the bedroom for a few minutes and returned wearing a red silky nightgown under an old flannel bathrobe decorated with faded pink flowers. Brueggeman glanced at her and looked back at the screen.

Now the monster was heading for the church. His shadow loomed across the white adobe walls, across a carved wooden crucifix, across the somber face of the handsome young priest. The mouth of the heroine opened into an O, and then an advertisement for sleeping pills came on.

Now, Brueggeman saw, Lena had Pootzie's forepaws up on her lap; she was rubbing his ears and whispering indecipherable endearments that made the dog groan with happiness. She looked into Pootzie's eyes and let him kiss her with that big pink elastic tongue of his. Across her face it went—over her chin, over her cheeks, even across her open mouth.

Brueggeman turned away in disgust. Earlier Lena had told him that Pootzie had to be restrained from eating from the cats' litter box. The sight of this animal licking her mouth sobered him instantly. He dropped into the ashtray on the coffee table the burnt-out joint he had been holding and went out to the kitchen to make himself a cup of coffee.

While he waited for the water to boil he opened the window and stuck his head out into the cold air. He had drunk too much and smoked too much; he felt woozy and stupid, and, looking out the window at the dirty snow, the dumpster beside the alley, the rusting bicycle frame chained to the fence, he wondered how life had managed to cast him up, however temporarily, on such a wretched shore, and how Lena, too, had managed to be cast up here. After a few minutes, feeling chilled, Brueggeman closed the window and checked the coffee water. It was all boiled away.

He put more water on the stove and looked for the instant coffee. In the second drawer he came across a little pile of the letters he had written her years before. He glanced through a couple of them. One of them was the letter he wrote when he and Miriam went out to California for the first time: . . . *Lena— three thousand miles across the great continent, and what we'll find when we get to that far shore, or what we're looking for, I do not know;*

*but yet I know that what I feel for you will not diminish with that
distance, or with a distance vaster still, or with the vast dark distances of time . . . .*

Brueggeman shivered with embarrassment. What was
embarrassing was that he had meant it all. He had really
believed, then, that his love for her was real, and that all he had
been through with Miriam was something shallow, something
false. *If I could do it all over again—*, he started to think. But he
could not do it all over again. That was not one of the options.

He put the letter back where he had found it and located the
coffee in the cabinet under the sink. He brought his cup back
into the living room with him.

Lena had stopped kissing her dog and she had also,
Brueggeman noticed, moved one of the boxes of doughnuts to
the coffee table in front of her. He said nothing about this, but
sat down beside her and, drinking his coffee, tried to make
some sense out of the final minutes of the movie they had been
watching.

"What happened?" he asked her.

"I don't know. I think the priest did something."

"What?"

"Hit the monster on the nose with a crucifix."

"But why is the girl's mother there? I thought the monster ate
her up."

"I guess she just fainted."

Lena took the box of doughnuts from the coffee table and
put it on her lap and opened it. She smiled at him conspir-
atorially.

"Well, which kind shall we have first?"

"I thought you weren't going to have any."

"But don't they smell good?"

Brueggeman knew all along that she wouldn't be able to
resist, but even so her lack of will power disgusted him. He
watched her pluck out a giant cream-filled doughnut and hold
it up to her nose to savor the bouquet, and then without even
thinking about it he leaned across the couch and smashed the
doughnut into her face. Big flaky crumbs and gobs of the
cream filling fell into her nightgown, down between her
breasts, and onto her lap. When the dog came dashing over to

gobble up the crumbs Brueggeman kicked it in the ribs so hard that it did a complete somersault and crept off whimpering into a corner.

"My hand slipped," Brueggeman said.

Lena did not look at him. Her lip was quivering. She wiped some of the cream filling from the bridge of her nose and said, in a soft, apologetic voice, "I guess I really shouldn't eat so much."

*   *   *

Dear Miriam, he wrote a few days later. Dear Miriam, This may seem peculiar to you, but I am here in Westham visiting Lena, whom you may remember from when I was doing her portrait a few years back. She is out at work now. I am sitting here with one of her cats on my lap. Miriam, the peculiar thing is that although we have only been together a few days I have this feeling that I might wind up marrying Lena. I don't know how to explain this to you other than to say that I have a great longing for some source of gentleness in my life.

Miriam, I am almost certain that this would be the stupidest thing I have ever done, but I do have the feeling it might happen. That's why I'm writing you. You're the only one I can think of who's always given me sensible advice.

O Miriam, I know it has been a long time since you have heard from me, and I know it must seem as though you only hear from me when I'm in some sort of trouble. I just wish there were some way I could see you again and talk to you, even if only for an hour. I know this isn't possible and I know Al doesn't like for you to get letters from me (and I know I will probably not even send you this one)—but I do think about you so often, and god, I wish you were here to advise me.